Petals in the Ashes

*For Brenda, Hilary,
Pat, Terry and the
class of 1990*

First published in Great Britain in 2004 by Bloomsbury Publishing Plc
38 Soho Square, London, W1D 3HB

A CIP catalogue record of this book is available from the British Library

ISBN 0 7475 6461 2

All papers used by Bloomsbury Publishing are natural, recyclable products made
from wood grown in well-managed forests. The manufacturing processes
conform to the environmental regulations of the country of origin.

Typeset by Dorchester Typesetting Group Limited
Printed in Great Britain by Clays Ltd, St Ives plc

10 9 8 7 6 5 4 3 2 1

Petals in the Ashes

Mary Hooper

BLOOMSBURY

Chapter One

The Journey

'A saddler who had buried all his children dead of the Plague, did desire only to save the life of his remaining little child, and so prevailed to have it received stark naked into the arms of a friend.'

'Rouse yourself, Hannah,' Sarah said, shaking my shoulder a little. 'Tie your hair back . . . and can you not splash your face with water from the flask? We don't want to arrive at Milady's house looking like frowsy kitchen wenches.'

With a big effort I opened my eyes and looked at my sister, who was sitting on the opposite side of the carriage from me and holding the babe, Grace, asleep in her arms. I yawned hugely.

'And put your hand to your mouth when you yawn,' Sarah said, 'or Lady Jane will think we've no manners at all.'

But I just yawned again and closed my eyes, for the effort of trying to keep them open was too much. After nearly three days on the road and two nights at wayside inns, with Grace hungry most of the time and squealing like a piglet, neither the constant jolting, the clatter of hard wheels on rough road nor the continuous thud of horses' hooves could stop me from sleeping.

Dimly, as if from far off, I heard Sarah address Mr Carter, our driver. 'Is it much further now to Dorchester?' she called, but I could not hear his reply over the drumming and the rattling and the clanging.

London seemed further away than just three days' travel. Already everything was so different. When I peered out of the curtains of our carriage there were no corpses slumped in the streets, no crosses on doors, no screams of those enclosed within foetid houses and no death carts conveying raddled bodies to the plague pits. There were just fields and farm animals and the occasional village, and the endless dusty road which threatened to jolt us to bits before we ever arrived at our destination. Our lives in London, threatened by the monstrous plague which had stalked and caused the deaths of our friends and neighbours, seemed a great way off, as if it had all happened in another existence.

My dear friend in London, Abby, had been nursemaid in one of the houses of the nobility. When this house had fallen to plague and been shut up for forty days, one by one those within had succumbed to the sickness and died. Towards the end, only Abby – and Grace, the babe in her charge – had remained alive in there. When Abby, too, had contracted plague, the babe had been entrusted to our care. My sister Sarah and I had stolen her away from the house and, using the Health Certificates meant for Abby and her mistress, Mrs Beauchurch, were taking Grace to her aunt, her mother's sister, Lady Jane Cartmel in Dorchester.

I must have fallen asleep, because the next thing I knew Sarah was shaking my arm. 'Were you having a bad dream?' she asked. 'You were murmuring to yourself and twisting in your seat.'

I raised my head from where it had lolled forward and shivered. I *had* been dreaming and it had not been pleasant, for Abby had been standing before me as I'd last seen her, her body ravaged by plague sores, holding out little Grace for me to take. I had not seemed able to hold the babe, though, for as I had reached for her she had become small and slight, like a changeling child, and had slipped through my fingers and floated away on the air, and Abby and I had watched her glide past us and wept together.

'I dreamed of Abby,' I said to Sarah, my eyes filling with tears. 'And of Grace. I was trying to hold her, but she just floated away.'

Sarah looked at me with some pity. 'We've got Grace safely now,' she said, and gave a wry smile. 'No one who has heard her yells could doubt that.' She leaned across the carriage and stroked my arm. 'And Abby is at peace, with no pain and no plague. Perhaps she's even watching over us to make sure we're taking care of Grace.'

I nodded and sniffed back my tears. 'I'm worried that she may not be getting enough milk,' I said. Although we had obtained flasks of ass's milk, we knew, of course, that this was no substitute for a mother's milk. 'Mayhap there'll be a wet nurse at the big house so she can feed properly.'

'Of course there will,' Sarah said, nodding. 'Lady

Jane will have prepared for our coming. There'll be a proper nurse and a lady's maid and a nursery, and for all we know some little cousins for Grace to play with. The poor lamb needs clothes as well – all she has is that little cloth she's wrapped in.'

When we'd had Grace lowered from the window of her plague-torn house we'd made sure she'd been naked, so she didn't take any plague germs with her. We'd wrapped her in a soft linen sheet we'd brought with us, but we'd been tearing off strips of it for her napkins all along the journey, so that now it was one quarter the size.

'If the journey takes much longer we'll be tearing up our shifts for her,' I said.

Sarah moved on her seat towards me. 'Will you take her for a moment, Hannah, while I adjust my dress? Mr Carter said that we're nearly there and I want to look tidy.'

'Are we really there at last?'

Sarah looked out of the window. 'Almost. He said we'll know we're at our destination when we turn into a park which is planted with all manner of fine and rare trees.'

'And these must be them!' I said, for I could see that around us, on either side of the wide drive and as far as the eye could see, were many shapely and beautiful trees with leaves of gold, lime, emerald, amber and deepest plum.

I took Grace carefully, being sure that the small round head was cupped securely in my hand. She was a pretty babe, with delicate pale skin and thick dark hair, and her eyes were as blue as forget-me-nots. I'd never seen Mrs Beauchurch, her mother, but Abby had said that the babe took after her rather than Mr Beauchurch, whom she'd once described as a red-faced booby with a nose like a tomato. But both of Grace's parents were with God now, I reminded myself, and it was not meet that I should speak ill of the dead. Indeed, if Grace, once grown, should ever ask me what her father was like, I would lie and say that he was the very model of princely good looks with all elegant attributes known to man.

Our destination being close, I began to think about how we would be greeted by Lady Jane. 'Milady will certainly be very pleased to have her infant niece here safely,' I said to Sarah as she rose and, holding on to the carriage straps, tried to smooth the creases out of her gown. 'Do you think she will reward us?'

'Tush!' Sarah said reprovingly. 'We are not doing this for gain. There's enough reward in saving Grace's life and gaining safe passage out of London for ourselves.'

'Yes, but she may reward us as well . . .'

Sarah permitted herself a small smile. 'Yes, she may.'

'I wonder if she will keep us there as companions in the big house with her. Or do you think we will be made to live as servants?'

Sarah shrugged. 'I cannot guess. We don't know her circumstances or whether she has a big family and children of her own – or even what age she is.'

'But I'm sure she will be so grateful to us that she will treat us like family and give us lovely rooms with four-poster beds in her elegant house!'

'When we get there I shall sleep for a week, whatever our rooms are like,' Sarah said, rubbing the back of her neck. 'I swear I am black and blue with being bounced in this box.'

'Abby told me that the house is newly built,' I said, 'and that it has a room just for bathing in, with cold water and hot water coming from a tap in the wall.'

Sarah's eyes grew wide. 'Indeed! I have never heard of such a thing.'

After thinking on this wonder for a moment, my thoughts turned once more to London. And from there, of course, to Tom, my sweetheart. 'But how long do you think we'll have to stay in Dorchester?'

Sarah shrugged. 'Until we get word that London is free from the plague. When we hear that the king and his court have returned, then we'll know it's safe.'

'And then perhaps Milady will give us a grand carriage to travel back in, and we can visit Chertsey on the way and see our family!' I said. But we wouldn't stop there too long, I told myself, for I would be dancing on coals by then to get back to Tom.

'We must pray that Chertsey, and our family, remain safe from plague,' Sarah said, very serious. 'For they do say that what is suffered in London one year spreads out from there the next.'

I fell silent at this, for I could not bear to think of the plague spreading and my family contracting it . . . of my mother, father, brothers or sister being visited. Surely it was enough that around us in London so many had died that their corpses rotted in the streets for want of people to bury them? Hadn't everyone suffered enough?

'Highclear House!' Mr Carter called suddenly, and Sarah and I scrambled to the window to look out and see our new home.

When we saw it we both gasped, for it was very large and immensely grand, with tall white marble columns to each side of the entrance, and steps going upwards to the doors. It had a great gravelled drive which swept across the front of the house with a fountain in its centre, and the water from the fountain rose into the air in a sparkling flume, catching the sunlight and making a rainbow.

I gazed at it in wonder, thinking that I had never seen a house more noble than this in my life before, nor a sight prettier than the rainbow in the fountain.

'I did not realise it would be so grand!' Sarah said, when we had stared and marvelled and found our voices again.

'And we have only the clothes we stand up in!' I wailed, trying to pull back my unruly hair and straighten my cap with my one free hand. 'I didn't even wear my best gown. I should have worn my green taffeta!'

The carriage came to a standstill and, as if knowing she was at her new home, Grace awoke and immediately began struggling to sit up. Anxious to be out of the carriage, I leaned forward to open the door. Sarah, however, motioned to me to sit back.

'Let Mr Carter do it,' she said. 'It's what he's used to.'

And so we waited while Mr Carter climbed down from his high seat and tied up the reins of the horses, then came to open the carriage door for us and lower the steps. Sarah got out first and I handed Grace to her, then I climbed out myself and gazed about me. The house in all its beauty stood before us, backed by more trees and a great park and, far off, what looked like a lake. Lady Jane's husband, I thought, must be monstrous rich.

'What shall we do now?' I whispered to Sarah, taking Grace back from her. 'Go and knock at the door?'

'I don't know,' Sarah answered, looking troubled.

We thanked Mr Carter for his great care in bringing us here, and he bade us farewell and began to lead the horses and carriage across the drive and towards the back of the house. A moment later the great doors opened and a woman dressed in black ran down the steps of the house.

'Mrs Beauchurch!' she called, with something like joy in her voice, and then she reached us and stopped. 'Oh, you are not . . .'

'No. No, indeed,' Sarah said, while I stood awkwardly, not knowing if I should curtsey to this woman, or indeed if she should curtsey to me. Was this a maid – or was it Lady Jane? Indeed, I thought it was not Lady Jane, for this woman was dressed quite modestly in a black moiré of half-mourning, with just one row of pearls around the high, ruffled neckline.

'Is she not with you?' The woman peered into the windows of the carriage as it moved away.

'No, we . . .' Sarah looked at me helplessly, but I did not know what to say, and so pretended to be very much occupied in keeping little Grace quiet. We had not thought of this: that those in Dorchester might not know that their relatives in London had died, and that strangers were bringing Grace to them.

'Mrs Beauchurch is . . . is not with us,' Sarah said hesitantly. She indicated Grace. 'But this is her child.

We have brought her from London.'

Hearing the word 'London', the woman took two steps backwards, and I noticed that she made a little hiccupping noise.

'But we are quite well and healthy!' I added quickly.

'May we speak with Lady Jane?' Sarah asked and, without another word, the woman turned and ran back into the house, leaving us standing outside as if we were peddlers selling ribbons.

For some minutes we just stood there, waiting. Grace began crying fitfully but I walked with her to the fountain to soothe her. She watched the water droplets falling and was amused by them, holding out her hands as if to catch them and making baby noises.

'Hannah!' Sarah called to me suddenly and, when I turned, another woman was coming out of the house with the woman in black.

This, we knew straightaway, must be Lady Jane. Although not tall, she was imposing, with fair hair caught on top of her head and styled into a hundred tiny curls. She was wearing a fashion that I'd seen worn by the quality in London: a cerise flowered silk dress cut low in front, with much gold lacing above the waist, slashed open to show a froth of petticoats. She carried a posy of flowers which she was to sniff throughout the time she spoke to us.

Instinctively, Sarah and I both curtseyed as she reached us.

'Who are you?' she asked sharply.

This was not the welcome we had hoped for, and we hardly knew how to begin our reply.

'Where is my sister? Where is Mrs Beauchurch?' she asked, speaking accusingly, as if she thought we might have stolen her from the carriage and made use of it ourselves.

'Were you not expecting us?' asked Sarah.

'I was expecting my sister,' came the reply. 'I sent Carter with my carriage and he's been waiting some two weeks for her fever to subside so he could bring her out of London.'

'She is . . . ' Sarah began, but I interrupted.

'The letter!' I urged her. 'Give Lady Jane the letter.'

Sarah looked at me, and then she delved into the canvas bag she was carrying. 'This letter,' she said, holding it out, 'is from your sister. You will recognise her hand.'

Lady Jane and the other woman stepped back together. 'I will not touch it!' said Lady Jane. 'Read it to me please, if you are able.'

'I am able,' Sarah said, adding gently, 'and I am very sorry for what you are about to hear.' She then read out the letter, which had been given to me by Abby.

'Dear Hannah,
I beg and beseech you in the name of the Almighty that you take my child, Grace, upon receipt of this letter, and carry her with all speed to my sister the Lady Jane at Highclear House, in Dorchester. My child is lusty and hearty now, but if left in this house of death she will surely perish. There are Certificates of Health for you and your sister, but you must travel under the names of Abigail and myself. A carriage has been procured and will be at the sign of the Eagle and Child in Gracechurch Street each day awaiting your arrival. The driver is

14

my sister's man and has a Certificate to travel.

On reaching Dorchester, Lady Jane will ensure that you and your sister are well cared for. You will be permitted to stay until the visitation has left London, when you will be given safe passage back.

May the prayers of a mother melt your heart and you find it within yourselves to grant my dying wish and save my child.

By my hand this 30th day of August 1665.
Maria Beauchurch.'

As Sarah reached the end of the letter, Lady Jane's face grew pale and her mouth tightened with distress. She shook her head to and fro several times, but did not speak.

'I am Hannah, and this is my sister, Sarah,' I said into the long silence which followed. 'Abby was Mrs Beauchurch's maid and was also my dear friend. She . . . she died of the plague.'

'As did your sister, shortly after writing this letter,' Sarah said gently. 'And her husband being already dead, we secured the safety of Grace and brought her to you, as she wished.'

Lady Jane's face did not change, but she took several more sniffs of her nosegay.

'Grace would have been alone in the house in London,' I said. 'She would have died.'

'I did not know of this,' Lady Jane said at last. 'I sent a messenger to the house to bring me news, but he did not return.'

'London is devastated by the sickness,' Sarah said. 'People are dropping like leaves from trees.'

'Eight thousand died last week alone,' I said. 'Your

messenger may have caught the sickness too.'

'But little Grace is well and lusty,' Sarah went on, 'although we are woefully inadequate at feeding her and hope to discover that you have a wet nurse here.'

'Wet nurse!' Lady Jane said scornfully. 'How would you expect me to find a wet nurse for a child, however well-born, that is come from a house where plague has taken its mother and father?'

'But Grace is healthy,' Sarah protested. 'As healthy as we are. See!'

She lifted Grace towards Lady Jane, who made agitated movements with her arms and moved away from us. 'No! Get back!'

'We have Certificates signed by the Lord Mayor himself,' I said, and then realised how stupid a statement that was.

'They are not in your names!' said Lady Jane immediately. 'They verify the health of my sister and her maid – and how little they are worth may be judged by the fact that both are now dead!'

'But for pity . . .' I held up Grace for her to see. 'Here is your niece and she is a beautiful child.' My voice shook, for not only did it seem that the lavish welcome I'd been expecting was not going to be forthcoming, but it also looked as though we were going to be turned away. 'Surely you'll let us stay?' I cried.

Lady Jane was silent for some moments, causing me much anxiety, but at last she spoke.

'I will not turn you away entirely. Indeed, it pains me to keep my own flesh and blood from my side, but I have my household here to consider. You must be quarantined until I am sure that you have not brought

16

the sickness with you.'

'But we are well . . .'

'Please consider . . .' Sarah began, but her voice trailed away for, like me, she felt that to protest was useless. Lady Jane would have heard what the conditions in London were like and would know how the plague proliferated – and had I not told her myself of the numbers who'd died in the previous week?

'How could I live with myself if I were responsible for bringing the plague to Dorchester?' Lady Jane asked. 'No, to vouchsafe my family here, the three of you must go into a pestilence house for a period of isolation.'

Sarah gasped. 'Oh, not that!' she cried, and she moved closer and put her arm around me.

I felt tears of fright spring to my eyes. To go through all we had done, only to be sent to one of those beggarly, foul-smelling places where the Angel of Death kept constant watch beside each bed! It would have been better if we'd not journeyed here at all, but had taken our chances in London.

'And what of Mr Carter?' the woman in black asked Lady Jane. She had not spoken in all this time, just made more of the strange hiccupping noises. 'He has been living amongst the sickness in London too. Must he go to the pesthouse?'

'Carter was afflicted in the last outbreak twenty years ago,' Lady Jane said. 'He recovered and will not catch it again.'

'But . . . but where is there such a house?' Sarah asked. 'Where must we go?'

'There is a pestilence house for travellers located on the road into Dorchester,' Lady Jane said. 'You must stay there for forty days – until we are sure that you are not contagious.'

'But we sought to secure the life of Grace by bringing her here – how will she fare in such a place?' I asked. 'We have no milk for her, nor clothes or coverings. All she has is the sheet she lies in.'

'I will have the milch-ass call there, and you may have whatever comforts I can provide,' Lady Jane said. 'After forty days you may return to Highclear House.'

'We might be dead by then!' I said bitterly.

'And how will we get there?' Sarah asked, tears now running down her cheeks. 'Must we walk?'

'No. I shall arrange for Carter to convey you,' Lady Jane said. She turned and spoke some words to the other woman, who hurried off towards the stables. 'But now will you show me the babe once more?' she asked.

I felt like refusing, but did not dare. I held Grace out towards her, loosening the sheet so that Lady Jane could see her healthy complexion and strong limbs.

'She is very like my dear sister,' was all she said, and then she turned and began to walk back towards the house.

'Not a word of thanks,' Sarah said as we watched her go inside.

'And sent to the pesthouse for our reward! Shall we just run away?' I said desperately. 'We could hide in the woods somewhere or make our way into a town. Anything rather than go to a pesthouse!'

Sarah shook her head wearily. 'How could we run away? We have no food nor means of shelter. Where would we go?'

'We have some money . . .'

'But not enough to last. And what of Grace – we couldn't live like animals in the woods with a child of such a tender age. Besides,' she added, 'I am so weary that I could not run anywhere.'

'So you mean for us to go to the pesthouse and live among the beggars?'

'I fear we have no choice,' she said. 'We must make the best of it.'

Chapter Two

The Pesthouse

'This month is the first decrease we have yet had in the Sickness since it began, and great hopes that the next month it will be greater.'

Upon the door of the pesthouse being opened, the first thing which arrested our senses was the stench which derived from it, as thick and foul as the miasma which had hung over London. It told of filth and rotting food and excrement and uncleansed bodies and was enough to turn the strongest stomach. Sarah and I both gagged and would have backed out again, but the parish officer, in whose charge we had been put, was close behind us.

As our eyes grew accustomed to the dim light inside, we looked about us, quaking with fear. Sarah had Grace in one arm and she and I linked hands and held on to each other like lifelines.

After the smell, the next most apparent things were the gloom – for it seemed as dark as a burying vault – and then the decay. No covering or cloth hanging relieved the rough walls or cobweb-encrusted beams, and the windows were high and narrow, with no glass in them. The floors were of trodden earth and littered with all manner of disgraceful objects: old, stained plaisters and blood-soaked bandages, full chamber pots, tattered cloths and rags, and what looked to me like the detritus and waste left behind by a dozen different plagues. Amidst this filth stood perhaps eight beds, some five supplied with a patient, either sitting or lying down, and covered with a grimy sheet or rough blanket.

'It is . . . foul,' Sarah said faintly, and she loosened her hand from my grip and pressed a white holland kerchief to her mouth to breathe through. She turned to the parish officer, Mr Beade, a rank and ratty-faced man with a good many pox scars. 'My sister and I are gentle born,' she said in a low voice. 'Is there not another place we may lie?'

I indicated Grace. 'This child is Lady Jane's niece,' I said. 'It is surely not right that she should be in such a place.'

'But Lady Jane herself has sent you,' he said, looking astonished that anyone should question the desirability of living there, 'and she will pay me for accommodating you and letting you wait out your quarantine. Come,' he went on, 'the time will go quickly, and with God's grace you will be out of here as healthy as you came in.'

Sarah and I exchanged despairing glances.

'And such pretty wenches – and you with your flaming locks!' he said, sliding his eyes to me. 'Two such frisky creatures will gladden the hearts of some of our poor patients!'

I gave him a hard stare at this, for I had no

21

intention of being a form of entertainment for the other inmates. 'May my sister and I at least stay close to each other?' I asked.

Sarah nodded. 'And, as we have a young child, may we have a corner or recess where we can attend to her needs and not disturb those who suffer here?'

Mr Beade – who was as ill-smelling as his pesthouse – looked doubtful.

'We are not seeking special treatment,' I said. 'We are thinking of the comfort of your patients as much as ourselves. The babe wakes frequently for milk and cries as often as any other infant.'

After much deliberation, and after dragging a poor person who looked half-dead from their mattress and moving them elsewhere, Mr Beade found a bed in the corner for Sarah, with my bed at an angle from this, thus enclosing Grace within the small square made by our two bedsteads. For her (no doubt wanting to secure the good opinion of Lady Jane), he procured an empty drawer from the adjoining almshouse where he lived, saying we could fill it with whatever material we wished and it would make a fine cradle.

Sarah looked around at the patients. 'Do any here have the plague?' she asked him in a low voice.

He shook his head. 'No, indeed!' he said. 'No one has the plague here. There is no plague in Dorchester.'

She pointed around us. 'Then what . . .?'

'Two have the spotted fever,' he said, 'one the bloody flux and one suffers the sweating sickness. One other is come back from London to Dorchester, which is their home town, and must sit out forty days, as you do.' Saying that, he went off about his duties, which seemed mostly to consist of chivying people to bestir themselves and not lie around succumbing to whatever ailed them.

'It is certain that at least one of them will have plague, whatever he says,' Sarah warned me as he left us. 'We must keep apart from those abed as much as we can.'

'Of course,' I said. I surveyed the grim scene before me and then sat down on the bed which had been allotted to me, for I suddenly felt very weary and tearful and wanted nothing more than to lie and weep a while.

Sarah immediately hauled me to my feet. 'The person who was lying on this bed before you looked like to die at any time!' she scolded me. 'We must gather some fresh straw to stuff our mattresses before we lie on them.'

I sighed, for I felt so careworn that right then I did not give a jot what infections I caught. I felt, too, that niceties such as fresh straw were useless, for I knew already that the plague respected neither person nor precaution, and would touch or leave whomever it pleased at its whim. However, on Sarah's insistence, we took our mattresses outside and emptied their contents on to a pile of refuse just by the door, which stank very badly and was buzzing with all manner of flies. The soiled covers we could do nothing about, but we shook them in the air and then filled them with dried grasses and heather (for the pesthouse was built on a common and there was much of this type of material around) before taking them back inside.

By the time we'd finished these tasks, Grace was crying fit to raise the Devil and this led us to a new dilemma, for the flask of milk we'd obtained from the inn where we'd stayed the previous night was now empty. On applying to Mr Beade, however, and emphasising to him how important it was that Lady Jane's niece should thrive, he sent his wife to a house on the other side of the common and, quite soon (while Sarah and I took it in turns to try and pacify Grace by walking round and round outside the pesthouse with her), a young girl came up leading an ass, which she proceeded to milk into an enamel jug.

Thus provided, we fed Grace using the same method that Abby had employed – trickling the milk down our fingers and letting it drop into her mouth – and left the rest of the milk, covered, in a shady place for later. We then took Grace inside and changed her undercloth, using another strip of the sheet, and made her as comfortable as possible on a nest made of hay in the drawer. As we were monstrous hungry ourselves by this time (for we'd not eaten since breaking our fast at the inn that morning) I went to find Mr Beade to ask how we got on for food, and what time it would be supplied.

The man fell to laughing in an uncivil way. ''Tis not a tavern!' he said. 'Do you think then to order yourself a dish of roasted pigeons or some grouse soup?'

'But how do we eat?' I asked him.

'My patients have food sent in by kindly neighbours living hereabouts,' he said. 'I'm sure Lady Jane will have something sent over in good time. In the meantime you may help yourselves to the leavings of what's already been provided.'

I went to tell Sarah this, and she pointed to a sturdy deal table at one end of the room. 'I think there are some scraps there,' she said. 'See what's left for us.'

I went to look and, shuddering, reported to Sarah that there was a small piece of green cheese, two hunks of hard bread and some dried-up cooked potatoes.

Sarah looked at me ruefully.

'But we cannot eat any of that!' I said, looking over to the table in disgust. 'We will starve.'

'No, indeed we will not,' Sarah said. 'We have two gold coins left, and if no food arrives from Lady Jane, we will ask Mr Beade to purchase food for us.'

'But what about today . . .'

'Today we will have to eat the potatoes and the bread,' Sarah said. 'It is not what we're used to but it will not harm us.'

I shuddered again.

'We must keep our strength up and our hopes,' she went on. She sat down on the bed and took my hands in hers. 'For didn't your sweetheart tell us that a merry heart does good like a medicine?'

I could not but smile at this, for it warmed me to hear Tom referred to as my sweetheart again and to remember what his master, the apothecary Doctor da Silva, had told him at the height of the plague.

We did not have to force down the stale bread, however, for as I turned to go back to the table and select the least objectionable items, a woman's voice called, 'Young ladies! I have a nicer loaf and would be glad to share it with you.'

This call, I was relieved to see, did not come from one of the half-dead who were lying prone, but from a woman who had just entered the pesthouse. She came over holding a loaf wrapped in a cloth, and I glanced over at Sarah, for I didn't know if I should accept it or not. The woman pressed it into my hands before I could decline, however. 'My family are nearby and keep me well supplied with food while I am here,' she said in a soft country voice. 'I can easily spare you this.'

I think Sarah might have wanted to keep both the woman and her bread at some distance, but it did not seem kindly to do this (and besides, I was very hungry), so, thanking her heartily, I bade her sit down beside us.

Our benefactor was a woman of perhaps thirty, with a round, honest face and a bird's nest of hair on which a battered white cap was perched. She was rather grubby and her apron was stained, but this was not surprising, for I did not anywhere see a wash bowl or any water where she could have cleaned herself.

'I'm Martha Padget,' she said, 'and I came from London some three weeks ago.'

I told her our names and said that we had just arrived from London that day. 'And the babe here is named Grace,' I said.

'She is your child?' Martha asked Sarah with some curiosity.

'No, indeed not!' Sarah said hastily. 'She is an orphan and the niece of Lady Jane Cartmel, who lives nearby.'

'Lady Jane!' Martha said, her eyes round.

'You know of her?'

'Of course,' Martha said. 'She is a great lady and known to everyone in Dorchester.'

'She may be a great lady,' I said bitterly, 'but she made us come to *this* foul and stinking place!'

'Hush!' Sarah said to me, and then added to Martha, 'We thought to be staying with Lady Jane – and indeed we might in the future, but first we have to live out forty days here.'

'As I do,' Martha said. She sighed. 'But tell me, does the plague rage in London as fiercely?'

'Ever worse,' Sarah nodded. 'The death cart is never absent from the streets.'

Martha shook her head. 'I fear London may become completely abandoned. All in my house perished: master, mistress, children and servants too. I was the cook – and thanks be to God that I was spared! I obtained a Certificate of Health and travelled back to Dorchester, for this is my home town and where my sister lives.'

'And how do you fare here in the pesthouse?' I asked.

She gave a shudder. 'I speak to no one, eat nothing that my sister does not provide and keep apart from those who have any fever. I have nineteen days to go before I can be released.' Grace murmured in her sleep and Martha got up to look at her, smiling kindly on her repose as people do with a babe. 'But what of you?' she asked.

I hesitated and Sarah gave me a warning look, but of course I would not say that we had travelled on false Certificates. 'When Grace's mother died, my friend Abby had care of the babe,' I said, 'but then she . . . she too was taken ill of the sickness, and she bade us take Grace away. We obtained Health Certificates, had a carriage to convey us, and arrived at Highclear House just this morning.'

'Were you in service in London?' Martha asked.

27

Sarah shook her head. 'We have a sweetmeat shop at the sign of the Sugared Plum in Crown and King Place.'

'We sell frosted rose petals and sugared fruits.' I looked around. 'It is different indeed from this frowsy place!' All the time I'd been speaking I had, unthinkingly, been breaking the soft bread between my fingers and putting small chunks in my mouth. Normally I would not have dreamed of eating bread without a preserve on it, or at least dipping it in sugar water, but being starving I found I did not miss these garnishings at all. Indeed, I think I might have eaten the whole of it, but I suddenly remembered Sarah and, with an apology, hastily passed her the rest.

Sarah, after thanking Martha for her kindness in supplying us with the bread, asked in a low voice if anyone in the pesthouse had died in the time she had been living here.

'Two,' Martha said. 'A week apart. And it was the plague that took them, for sure. I know the signs as well as anyone who has been in London. An old crone came in, however, one who had been employed as a searcher of the dead, and gave out that the first had died of French pox and the second of the bloody flux.'

'Why was this?' Sarah asked.

'Because Mr Beade would not have it any other way,' Martha said, after looking over her shoulder to make sure that he was not nearby. 'He is employed to keep the plague out of Dorchester, and that is what he does. He keeps out the plague by not allowing any mention of it.'

'So – forgive me – but why have you not caught it?' Sarah asked.

Martha shrugged. 'Why not indeed? I spend most of my days out of doors – but if I knew why some catch plague and some do not I would bottle it and make myself a fortune!'

'We try to chew a sprig of rosemary every day – and we each have a talisman in our pockets and took a cordial when we were in London,' I said, 'but which of these helped us we don't know.'

While we were speaking we became aware that Mr Beade was outside, speaking to someone and employing a good deal of bluster and affability. A bit after this he called to me and Sarah, saying that a small crate had arrived for us from Lady Jane, with a message that the rest of the pesthouse was to benefit from anything that we didn't require.

In some excitement, Sarah and I took in the crate and, lifting the lid, discovered some linen sheets, patched but very clean and soft, a quilt, some gloves, three dresses (which were rather out of fashion but, judging by the quality of the lace, her Ladyship's own) and several cotton smocks and petticoats, as well as face cloths, a towel and a small bar of soap. Grace was supplied with some two dozen napkins, a quantity of smocked and tucked gowns, two loosely-knitted shawls and some pretty bonnets with ribbons. As well as these things, there was a basket containing two fresh loaves of bread, some wine, a whole round cheese and some fruit: one orange and a great many apples and plums.

The note with the crate said:

Mistress Hannah and Mistress Sarah. Lady Jane has bade me send you these items which she hopes will

go some way towards making your stay at the pesthouse a less irksome one. I will ensure you receive adequate amounts of food, and please apply to me at any time if I may supply further items for your needs, and be assured that I am your diligent and faithful servant,
R. Black,
Housekeeper to Lady Jane Cartmel

Even the fact that we had heard Mr Beade exclaiming over the crate a while before and were certain that he had already helped himself to a few items, did not detract from our pleasure. We immediately set to changing into the clean undersmocks and dresses (for we had travelled four days in the same things) and asked Mr Beade for a washing bowl, that we might wash both ourselves and our undergarments. Before we did these things, we pinned up one of the sheets across the end of Sarah's bed so none could see us undressing. We must preserve our modesty, Sarah said, adding, 'Although the rest of the inmates look half dead, you cannot be too sure.'

Although the ordeal to be endured in the pesthouse still seemed very wearisome, we felt a deal better after the supply of these items and the knowledge that we would receive regular food. We knew our friendship with Martha would help, too, for she was a good source of information both on pesthouse conduct and on Mr Beade.

Over the next few days, with our new friend's help, we began to clean up the ill-smelling place. Already there was a nurse of a kind who called daily to see how the bedridden fared, but now we asked that a maid be sent in to keep the floor swept clean, and also to wash the mattress covers and change their contents regularly so that the air would smell sweeter. We had the pile of refuse moved from outside the front door to a good way off, strewed herbs on the floor and indeed employed most of the methods that had been decreed in London to prevent the plague from spreading. We asked that, unless a person was on the verge of death, everyone should go outside and use the privy for their business, for it was not at all decent that chamberpots be used and left under the beds for days on end, especially as the weather continued very warm.

The weather, indeed, was a blessing to us, for if it had rained we would have been forced to stay inside the pesthouse amid the foul vapours and humours. As it was, though, we spent a good deal of our time in the walled garden which surrounded it, separating it from the hamlet beyond. We asked for paper and pencils to be sent and amused ourselves by gathering herbs and any flowers we could find and pressing and naming them, and also taught Martha the basics of the alphabet and how to form her name, for she had never been to school.

We kept Grace outside as much as possible, and she thrived on country air and grew plump on fresh ass's milk, especially when a bone feeding-cup with spout arrived in one of the regular deliveries from Highclear House. This enabled her to drink more milk and at her own pace, for she quickly learned to gulp from it and bang it on the floor when she wanted it refilled. Sarah had more patience with Grace than I and spent longer in her company for, although I loved her dearly, to tell the truth I had seen rather too much of my three little brothers mewling and puking to have any great affection for infants. One of the inmates of the pesthouse carved a little wooden poppet for her, and Sarah and I made dresses and bonnets for it from scraps of sheeting (although Grace, who was teething, ignored these coverings and just gnawed at the dolly's head).

Some two weeks or so after we'd arrived in the pesthouse, Martha was seen by a doctor from Dorchester, pronounced fit, and allowed to go on her way. We knew we would miss her very much, but we promised that we would see each other again – and indeed she said she could not wait to visit us in Highclear House.

One person died over the next week (it was given out that he'd died of spotted fever) and two more people were admitted for quarantine: an old man and his son. They too had come from London and brought the welcome news that at last there had been a downturn in the numbers dying from plague. From a tragic high of ten thousand deaths in one week, the numbers had gradually fallen. The first week in October showed three thousand, with further falls expected.

'We must write to our family,' Sarah said, on learning this news. 'Now the numbers of dead are decreasing, they may allow a letter through.'

I nodded. 'Besides, we are not writing from London, but from Dorchester, and that will make a difference.'

We deliberated a good while on what to say about

the death of Abby, for Abby's mother, a widow, lived just a short distance from our house in Chertsey and would not yet have heard of it. We did not know if we should put our own mother in the difficult position of passing on the news.

In the end we decided we would not mention it, for neither our mother nor father could read well, and it would have been too difficult to explain the circumstances of Abby's death and to say how we had taken over the care of little Grace and brought her to Lady Jane. Accordingly, we just wrote the following:

Dearest Mother and Father,
We trust that you remain in good health as we do, thanks be to God. You will have no doubt heard of the unhappy conditions in London at present and we write to tell you that due to certain circumstances we are at present staying in Dorchester. On our journey back to London we shall be sure to visit you, and in the meantime send love to John, George, Adam and Anne, and remain your loving daughters, Sarah and Hannah

Folding the parchment and sealing it with wax supplied by Mr Beade, we sent it care of the Reverend Davies at our parish church in Chertsey, trusting that he would pay the necessary small sum to take delivery of it and pass it to whichever member of our family came to church the following Sunday.

'Imagine the excitement when it is received!' Sarah said fondly.

I nodded. 'Anne will carry it back home to Mother . . .'

Sarah laughed. 'And John and George and little Adam will fight to see it first . . . and they will try to read the words . . . and Mother will show them their own names at the end.'

'And then the boys will practise their writing by making a fair copy underneath!'

We were silent for a good while after this, and I felt very low and as if I could weep. Though it was only five months since I'd seen my family, a great deal had happened to me in that time, and I wished most desperately to be back safely in our little thatched cottage in Chertsey with them all.

When our forty days had elapsed, Mr Beade applied for the local doctor to call and examine us. He did so and pronounced the three of us fit and healthy. He must have then supplied the same information to Highclear House, for that afternoon the coach which had conveyed us from London to Dorchester called at the pesthouse and Mr Carter, bowing, requested that we collect up our belongings, as Lady Jane wished to receive us.

Immediately, very excited, we dressed Grace in her best dress and bonnet, attended to our hair and gowns and made ourselves ready for the short journey. Mr Beade, whose person who had not been part of the pesthouse improvements and who still stunk worse than a polecat, ran beside the carriage for some distance, seemingly sorry to see us go.

'Don't forget, ladies, to tell Lady Jane how I have nurtured and taken especial good care of you!' was his last cry to us.

Chapter Three

Highclear House

'Called at my booksellers for a book writ about twenty years ago in prophecy of this year coming on, 1666, explaining it to be the Mark of the Beast.'

The contrast between Highclear House and the pesthouse could not have been more marked. We had first seen Highclear in the sunlight so that the marble columns gleamed and the windows glittered silver, and though when we returned it was raining, with storm clouds above as thick as pease pudding, the sight of it was still enough to make you catch your breath. It was imposing and stately, with something of the grandness of the Royal Exchange about it, and looked far too splendid to be a house built merely for people to live in.

Mr Carter drove us around to the back, past a chapel, brewhouse, laundry, stables, and coach houses. There seemed enough of these buildings to form a small village, and this impression was strengthened by the large number of people we saw going about their duties: clerks, maids, grooms, valets

– even two reverend gentlemen.

The carriage stopped in a paved courtyard and, alighting, we entered the house through a heavy oak door and went down steps into the kitchen. This was a room as big as an alehouse, its walls lined with pot cupboards and shelves. Along one wall was a vast black-leaded cooking range, and above this were two complete rows of shining copper pots, pans and moulds. There were several deep pewter sinks and two fireplaces, each holding a roasting animal turning on a spit, and the bright flames of the fires reflected off the lines of copper pans, making the whole room cheerful. Indeed it looked so warm and welcoming that for some moments we just stood there staring about us, for it was such a contrast to the dark and dirty aspect of the pesthouse where, in spite of all our efforts, rats scuttled across the floor at night and lice and fleas bit us into wakefulness, that I felt I could scarce look at it enough.

Grace, secure in my arms, was silent and wide-eyed too, and the several women in white aprons who were busying themselves about the room smiled at her – and us – in a friendly manner. We were both astonished and delighted to see that one of these women was our friend Martha from the pesthouse: Martha in a long white apron, her unruly hair pushed up and almost hidden under a new starched cap.

'I've been waiting for you!' she said, coming up and kissing us in turn. 'Mrs Black told Cook that you would be arriving here one day this week.'

'But what are you doing here?' I asked, very surprised.

'Well, my sister has a new husband and I could not

abide him,' she said. 'I heard that her Ladyship wanted a cook-maid and so I applied, knowing that you would be coming here soon.'

She stroked Grace's cheek and the babe, recognising her, began to babble at her in nonsense baby-talk. Meanwhile, I still stared around the room in awe, for here was a grand home, a stately home, such as I'd never entered before. Through a doorway I could see into a still room, where thick bunches of dried flowers and herbs were hanging, and another doorway led into a buttery, with vats of cream and butter standing by to set. I wondered about the rest of the house and concluded that if I was in such great awe at the kitchen, I might possibly be struck dumb by all the rest of it.

'What are we to do here – do you know?' I asked Martha, for Sarah and I had often talked about how we might be received by Lady Jane and what she would do with us.

'What will be our status?' Sarah added.

Martha shook her head. 'I have no idea,' she said, 'for though we maids keep our ears pricked for gossip, we rarely hear anything of merit. The undercook is above me, and the cook is above her, and the housekeeper is above us all. I have never even seen Lady Jane! I do know that Lord Cartmel is something to do with Parliament, but he's away in Oxford where they're sitting.'

'Why sitting in Oxford?' Sarah asked.

'Because of the plague still being in London,' Martha replied, dropping her voice on the dread word.

'But we did hear that the numbers of dead were

37

falling,' I said.

Martha nodded. 'They say there's an improvement now the cooler weather is come. Thanks be to God,' she added.

Grace made a grab for Martha's cap and pulled it sideways and I moved her on to my other hip and so away from temptation. 'Is this a good house to work in?' I asked.

'It is,' Martha assured us, 'for although Mrs Black is strict, she's fair. And it's most beneficial to the staff that the poor lady suffers permanently from—'

But she did not continue, for just then there was a strange little noise from the doorway and a moment later the woman in black we had first spoken to some forty days before appeared. This was, in fact, Mrs Black (which name I thought most appropriate for someone wearing such sombre clothing), housekeeper to Lady Jane. As such, she supervised all the female staff: cooks, maids, governesses, needlewomen and launderesses.

Another moment and we were to find out what Martha had been about to tell us of Mrs Black, for as she came towards us she hiccupped twice, tiny movements which jerked her head back and caused a little inward breath. I felt a laugh rising inside me but managed to keep it down, for Mrs Black was holding out her arms for Grace.

'At last! You are welcome to Highclear House,' she said, adding, 'and indeed the little one is more than welcome.'

Sarah and I both bobbed curtsies – I as well as I could, for Grace was plump and heavy now. Mrs Black took her from me and I think Grace might have

38

cried at being handled by a stranger, indeed she opened her mouth to start, but Mrs Black gave two more hiccups and Grace forgot to bawl, looking at Mrs Black with such an astonished expression that again I felt I wanted to laugh.

'You are to come upstairs now and speak to Lady Jane,' Mrs Black said, 'and be sure to say how very grateful you are for her kindness in receiving you here.'

Sarah and I exchanged brief glances and, as Mrs Black led the way through the kitchen, I said to her in a whisper that it should be the other way round: *she* should be grateful to *us* for rescuing Grace. Sarah shook her head at me to be quiet.

Mrs Black, hiccupping gently, led us down a long corridor, and through doors, and up and down short flights of stairs, and then said we were entering the part of the house where Lady Jane and her family lived.

Going through a door into this part of the house, the difference was apparent immediately. One moment we were in a narrow, dark stairwell without a rug under our feet, the next we had entered another world where the air was heady with the scent of pot pourri, and where we trod on thick, soft carpets and looked up to walls hung so generously with portraits, mirrors and tapestries that the wallpaper behind could scarce be seen.

'You will never be in this front part of the house again, except by invitation,' Mrs Black said, 'for the house has been designed so that the staff and the family lead completely separate lives. The servants here have their own staircases and corridors and are not seen by the family.'

Sarah and I both looked surprised at this, for we had never heard of such an arrangement before.

'It is so that the gentry walking up the main stairs in the morning do not see last night's chamber pots coming down to meet them,' Mrs Black said.

'And is there really a room for bathing,' I asked, 'in which the hot water comes out of a tap in the wall?'

'There is,' she said, 'but it means two maids working four hours each to fill the tank with hot water, so it has been used once only, and that after my Lady's last confinement.'

We paused outside a door gilded all over with carvings and Mrs Black shifted Grace into a more comfortable position and rubbed a smudge from her plump cheek, then looked at me and Sarah critically. 'Can you not calm your hair a little more?' she asked me. ''Tis all over the place like a storm.'

I adjusted my cap. 'It is tied at the back,' I said, turning slightly to show her. 'I fear it has a mind of its own, though.'

'And such a colour,' Mrs Black murmured. 'Do you not find it over-bright?'

I did, of course, and had tried many times to subdue its redness, but since finding out that Nelly Gwyn had hair of the exact same colour and type, I had begun to bear it a little better. Hearing someone criticise it now just caused me to run my fingers through my curls so that they stuck out further.

'Hannah's hair is much admired,' Sarah put in, hiding a smile. 'All the gallants comment on it.'

'There are no gallants here,' said Mrs Black dryly. She gave us a final look-over and brushed a leaf from

Sarah's skirt, then tapped at the door gently and ushered us into the room.

I just managed to stop myself gasping at the sight before me, and indeed I could not describe it in any detail, but knew that there were vast purple velvet drapes and many mirrors hung with crystal droplets and studded with candles (for the day was already dark), and that the whole effect was one of glitter and light and richness. Three golden bird cages hung from the ceiling, each with several brightly-coloured birds within.

In the middle of all this glory sat Lady Jane at cards with three other ladies around a small table. All four had high, glossy wigs and were dressed in the finest silks and satins: Lady Jane was in stiff gold brocade over gold moiré, one of her companions was in brilliant green silk lined with silver and the remaining two ladies were in pink: one deep plum, the other clover. The overall look was as rich and elegant as a painting.

The ladies put down their cards and stared at us, causing Sarah and I to sink unbidden into curtsies as deep as if we were faced with the King of England.

Lady Jane rose from the table and, ignoring us, made straight for Grace and took her from Mrs Black. She snatched her too abruptly, though, for she immediately began to cry.

'Hush, you minx!' Lady Jane said, then made an ineffectual try at pacifying Grace by lifting her into the air and swinging her about.

'She dislikes that!' I blurted out, and would have taken her back again but was somehow stopped by the glances of my sister and Mrs Black.

'Then pray take her, Mrs Black!' Lady Jane said, seeming to lose interest. 'I know you have her nursery all prepared.'

Dropping Grace into Mrs Black's arms, Milady sat down once again at the card table and it seemed that we were dismissed (and had as much value as fleas on a counterpane, I said to Sarah later). But Mrs Black delayed, nodding at us meaningfully.

'Oh! Thank you for your great courtesy in receiving us here in your house,' Sarah said.

Her Ladyship nodded and, as she glanced at me, I asked, 'What are we to do now?'

Mrs Black gave a hiccup and another hard look and I added, 'Your Ladyship. If you please.'

'You will both stay here, of course, until the plague leaves London,' said Lady Jane, picking up her cards and studying them intently. 'And then Carter will take you back there in the carriage.'

'But how will we know when it's all right to return?'

'We have news every week,' Lady Jane said, waving her hand dismissively. 'There are newspapers and letters now coming out of London – we'll know when it's safe.' She turned away from us back to her hand of cards and, as Mrs Black and Sarah were both in the doorway and making big eyes at me, I withdrew.

'Lady Jane must not be troubled by such as yourselves,' Mrs Black chided and hiccupped, once we were outside. 'She has more important matters to think on.'

'So we saw,' I murmured, but Mrs Black did not hear me above Grace's cries.

With Grace still bawling, Mrs Black led us through more corridors to the nursery wing, which she told us was where Lady Jane's children and their staff lived and were schooled. She explained that Grace was to have a room of her own and a nursery maid to tend her, and accordingly we entered a small, whitewashed room and found a young girl of perhaps fourteen blowing on some coals in the grate to try to get them to catch. This was obviously to be Grace's nursery, for as well as a narrow bed there was a stout wooden cradle and a table and chair, and also a wooden rocking horse which looked as if it had been well used by Lady Jane's children, being battered and having most of its mane missing.

The girl jumped to her feet as we appeared and gave a curtsey to each one of us in turn. Not used to being curtseyed to and unsure of what my reaction should be, I returned this compliment, although Sarah frowned at me.

'Anna here will have charge of Grace from now on,' Mrs Black said to us. 'She's a careful girl. Her mother died in childbirth so she's brought up her three little sisters on her own.'

Anna smiled shyly at us and then held out her arms for Grace, who'd gone silent as we'd entered the room but who'd now started crying again. Anna did not seem perturbed at this, though, but settled Grace into the crook of her arm and, with her other hand, popped something into her mouth. Grace immediately began to suck greedily.

''Tis a raisin tied in muslin,' Anna said. 'It always works.'

'Oh! We have left her poppet behind in the pesthouse!' I said, suddenly remembering Grace's dolly.

Mrs Black made a face of displeasure. 'She won't

need any dirty things from that place,' she said. 'She'll have all manner of fine toys and games from now on and will play nicely with her cousins. When she's mastered Dobbin there . . .' she nodded towards the make-believe horse, '. . . she'll learn to ride a real one.'

Although Grace's lips still moved in rhythm as she sucked at the muslin comforter, her eyelids had closed by the time we said our goodbyes. She looked so bonny and pretty as I bent to kiss her that I felt a great ache of sadness, for I had tended her like a mother for six weeks, and she was my last link to Abby. Feeling the tears well up I let out a small sob, which caused Sarah to begin to weep too, so that Mrs Black led us from the nursery in quite a gentle manner, telling us that we could visit Grace whenever we liked.

We were then shown to our room, which was quite plain, with an iron bedstead and several sets of shelves, and told by Mrs Black that as long as we kept to the back part of the house we could come and go from here as we liked. The only time our presence was essential was in the chapel every Lord's Day.

When Mrs Black had left, Sarah and I felt such a sense of relief that our ordeal at the pesthouse was over that we sat down together on our bed and wept, nor hardly stopped for the rest of that afternoon. We were weeping for all the horror we'd left behind in London, and for our friends who were dead, and for the relief in delivering Grace safely. On my part I was also weeping because of Tom, for I had a dreadful fear that I might never see him again.

Our time in Highclear House passed slowly, for we had no regular duties and it seemed that Lady Jane had forgotten about us. As we waited to hear that the plague had left London, weeks turned to months and the weather grew cold and frosty. We had a fireplace in our room and a weekly allowance of coal, and so spent a deal of time there either trying to improve our reading (there was a large library, though with monstrous dull books), embroidering our clothes or learning still-room recipes. Martha was skilled at these and showed us how to make pot pourri, scented washing waters and pomander balls. She also showed me how to make a herbal infusion with rosemary and lad's love to condition my hair and stop it being quite so unruly (although it did not subdue its redness). We occupied ourselves too by playing with Grace, and with the cats and dogs around the house, for in London we had not seen either of these for several months as they'd been put to death in case they spread plague.

We heard that the plague had moved from London to Sherborne, in Dorsetshire, where it was presently rife, and also to Southampton and the Isle of Wight. Mercifully, it continued to abate in London. We heard from *The Newes* (which arrived at Highclear every week and appeared downstairs a few days later), that in December there was a frost in London so hard that the Thames froze over and a Fair was held on it, and that this exceeding brutal weather had caused the numbers dying of plague to fall even more. *The Newes* informed us, however, that the king, the court and most others who'd fled still hesitated to return to the capital, not yet convinced that it was safe.

The regular servants in the house tolerated me and Sarah, although some, I felt, rather resented the fact that we had no real work to do. Their burden of duties was unceasing, and watching them – especially the housemaids – busying themselves from morn until it pleased their betters to let them retire at night, made me vow that I would never go into service.

We helped them occasionally, making sweetmeats and comfits for several of Lady Jane's musical evenings and again when there was a ball to mark his Lordship's return from Oxford. He arrived in a flurry of pomp just before Christmas, bringing a number of personal staff: a valet, butler, groom, footman, gentleman of the wardrobe and bootboy, which swelled the numbers below stairs even more.

The bootboy, I am ashamed to say (for he was a scurrilous little wretch), became somewhat attached to me and would follow me around the gardens when I was looking for feverfew – for this herb had many useful properties – or for herbs which might be turned into comfits, talking all the time and distracting me from whatever task I was set upon. As he listened at doors and was a great gossiper, however, we found out quite a lot of information from him. He told us that there was no plague at all in Oxford, and that the gentry did not spare much time to think of those who suffered in London.

'The only talk in Oxford is of Lady Castlemaine's imminent lying-in,' young Bill told me one morning when I was in the kitchen garden looking for winter-flowering herbs. 'There are those who say that it is not the king's child she bears.'

'Lady Castlemaine is at Oxford with the court?' I asked in surprise, for though we all knew who the king's mistresses were and spent many hours discussing their various merits and who was the most beautiful, I had not realised he took any away with him.

He nodded. 'The king has made Lady Castlemaine a Lady of the Bedchamber to the queen, so now she accompanies them everywhere.'

'The queen is there too?'

'She is – though nobody gives a tuppeny jot for her. It is Lady Castlemaine who has the power.'

'And is she very lovely?'

'I have only seen her at a distance,' Bill said, 'but they say she has fine eyes and a mane of hair that is all her own, and when she is in a room nobody looks at anyone but her.' He came close to me. 'But I daresay you could hold your own against her, Sweeting.' He put a grimy hand on my arm and his nails were so dark with boot-blacking and dirt that I gave a little scream and moved away.

'Tell me more about what it was like at Oxford,' I said hastily, pulling my plaid shawl around me against the wind. 'Do they really not care about those left in London?'

'They say they do,' he said, 'but I say they do not, for they continually hold balls and masques and entertainments. They say it is to keep their minds from the horror of the plague.'

'And do they talk of when they will move back?' I began, but we had heard a hiccup which meant that Mrs Black was close by, and Bill suddenly darted back towards the house, for Mrs Black had a sharp tongue and would not hesitate to report him to his master for slacking. I bent over the ground again, finding some rosemary growing between the cracks of paving and picking it.

'Ah,' Mrs Black said, gliding up to me, 'I was looking for either you or your sister, and Martha said you might be out here.'

'I'm looking for herbs,' I said.

'It was that of which I came to speak to you. Of . . . herbs and simples.'

'I have not much knowledge,' I said hastily, for I knew it did not do to be a woman and confess to understanding of these things, for a neighbour of ours in Chertsey had been bitten by a mad dog and had consulted a local wise woman who'd given him the herb plantain. When he'd later died, she'd been accused of witchcraft.

She hiccupped twice. 'You may have noticed this . . . my affliction.'

I nodded solemnly.

'I would have it treated, but I fear going to a doctor in case he tells me that I have something else. Something worse. Is there anything I can take? Any cordial you can make me for it?'

'I'm not sure,' I said. Sarah and I had written down various recipes and some cures which had been given to us by Doctor da Silva the apothecary, but I wasn't certain if we had anything which would cure hiccups.

'Perhaps you could ask your sister and then let me know,' she said.

I spoke to Sarah later that morning and we came to the conclusion that Mrs Black suffered so because she liked highly-spiced foods, so we looked through our writings and found several herbs which were said to be good for the digestion. All of these, unfortunately, only flowered in summer, but luckily we had preserved a few stalks of hawkweed, a useful herb with several medicinal properties, so we ground up the dry flowers and steeped them into a cordial. After sipping this mixture after meals for only two days, much to our surprise Mrs Black's hiccups ceased. She was so grateful to us that a whole extra pail of coal appeared in our room, and she also gave us five pairs of fine white kid gloves that Lady Jane had discarded.

However, having now lost notice of the housekeeper's imminent arrival anywhere, the other servants were not so grateful.

The Highclear Ball was held on the eve of the New Year: 1666, which was forecast and predicted to be a year of great import because of the triple occurrence of sixes. We discovered this from *Lily's Almanack*, which Cook had purchased, even though she could not understand much of the writing. When it was quiet or Mrs Black was occupied elsewhere, Cook would ask me to read from it so that we could learn what was to happen in the coming year, and also to tell her and the other servants their fortunes according to their astrological signs.

Late on the night of the ball we did this in the kitchen, sitting at the long table while the ball was going on over our heads, for, a great meal having been eaten in the dining hall earlier (and Mrs Black having retired to her own room), the staff were free to make merry. Indeed, some bottles of sack had been given for this purpose, and we had also been supplied with the carcasses of several roast capons, geese and pigeons which had been barely touched by the gentry above, so stuffed were they with the multitude of lavish dishes which had gone before.

I didn't fully understand what I was reading from the *Almanack*, and I didn't believe that many of the servants did either, but the most important prediction was that a momentous change would occur during this year, 1666. 'For in the Book of Revelation it says that 666 is the number of the beast,' I read out.

'Well, whatever does that mean?' Martha asked, and we all shook our heads.

'The beast is capable of bringing fire from heaven and causing the houses of the mighty to fall,' I continued, while everyone made wide eyes at each other, pretending to be affrighted.

The serious manner in which I presented this news to the servants was, however, somewhat spoilt when Bill came up with some mistletoe and, pulling me backwards off the table, tried to kiss me. I, screaming, ran helter-skelter across the kitchen with him in pursuit, locked myself in the dairy and only came out when he promised not to handle me so.

Later we all drank to the coming-in of the year, and Sarah and I hugged each other and said that we were grateful and relieved that the old year was over.

'Whatever happens in this one, it cannot be as cruel as the last,' she said.

I shook my head. 'Indeed it cannot!'

Chapter Four

Chertsey

'But now the Plague is abated almost to nothing, and I intending to go to London as fast as I can, my family having been there these two or three weeks.'

'Aren't we near yet?' I asked Sarah. 'We *must* be nearly there now.'

She looked out of the carriage window and into the sky to judge the position of the sun. 'Mr Carter said we would arrive near sundown,' she said. 'And we're a way off that yet.'

I sighed, long and loud. Never had a journey seemed so wearying. Even travelling from London to Dorchester seemed nothing to this, for we'd had Grace with us then and much to do in keeping her fed and pacified.

'We'll soon be there, Hannah.' Sarah smiled into the distance. 'And just think how excited the little ones will be to see us.'

'And Father will grunt a bit and nod and look pleased!'

'And then Mother, after she's got over her shock,

51

will cry with happiness that we're home.'

I nodded with satisfaction. All that. All that and more: Mother would have one of the boys catch a chicken and cook it for supper, with a flummery to follow that had been made with cream from our own cows. After we'd eaten we'd all sit down, light the candles and tell our news: Mother and Anne would want to know about the shop, what sweetmeats were most popular and the fashions worn by the quality who came to buy from us, while the boys probably would want to know how many bodies we'd encountered when the plague was at its height, and if we'd seen anyone with the buboes on them. Later, I would be sleeping once again in the bed-chamber where I'd been born, with the damp patch on the wall which was shaped like an oak tree, and Tyb, our big old cat, would sleep on my bed and wake me in the night by leaping around the room trying to catch moths. I was so longing to be there.

Our stay at Highclear House had continued until the numbers dying from plague on the London Bills of Mortality had come right down and it was considered perfectly safe for us to travel. We'd heard at the end of February that the king and his court had returned to Whitehall, but it had taken us some time to arrange our journey, as Lady Jane had by then gone out of England to stay with relations in France. Mrs Black, however (who could not do too much for us since we had cured her of the hiccups), had written to her mistress asking that Carter might take us in the carriage as far as Chertsey. Permission had been granted, and Sarah and I were to stay with our family for a week or two before we made the last stage of the journey to London by whatever means was convenient. We had bid farewell to the Highclear household, but had only been really sorry to leave Grace and our good friend Martha.

I stretched my legs in the cramped carriage, then lifted my skirt to rub at my knees. 'Every part of me has been jolted to bits,' I complained. 'I swear I am black and blue under my shift.'

Having rubbed at my aches, I pulled my skirt down again and patted the pleats carefully into place, for the material was costly and the colour vivid blue and I loved the gown dearly. By and large, Sarah and I had managed to obtain several new outfits during the time we'd been at the house. Lady Jane was generous with her cast-offs and, in addition, a bolt of deep plum linsey-woolsey had arrived from abroad, the colour of which Lady Jane had not liked, so she had passed it to Mrs Black. With her help, and that of the needlewoman at the house, Sarah and I had made skirts and matching jackets of it, which we later embroidered and which looked very fine.

We came to a crossroads and I peered out of the carriage window. There was a set of stocks here, and also a double gallows where the bodies of two highwaymen hung, swaying gently in the wind. This caused to make me think of Gentleman Jack, the highwayman who'd plied his trade around our home town and on the roads into London – a dashing figure always dressed in the finest silks and satins who oft stole a kiss from the ladies when he took their diamond rings. I asked Sarah if she thought he were still on the roads.

'I think not,' she answered. 'I am sure that our neighbour Mr Newbery said to me that he saw Gentleman Jack hung at Tyburn and his head stuck on a pole over London Bridge.'

I was just taking in this news when there was a shout from outside and a yell and swearing from Mr Carter, and one of our horses neighed and reared up, causing the carriage to skew across the road. I screamed, for it seemed obvious to me what had happened. 'It's highwaymen! We're going to be robbed!' I cried to Sarah.

I had no jewellery, but I immediately pushed my small bag under the seat so it was out of view. Our gowns and capes were in a chest on top of the carriage and they would be stolen straightaway, but at least they would not see my bag containing my own special things: brushes, pink kid gloves, a little silver box and two pretty fans.

Sarah, too, pushed her bag out of view, and tucked her only jewellery (a gold neck-chain that our grandmother had given her) into her neckline so that it was hidden.

There was another shout, but we were too frightened to lean out of the window for, apart from Gentleman Jack, most of the highwaymen were violent, lewd fellows who would shoot first and rob second, and think nothing of stripping a lady's dress from her and leave her standing in her shift. Indeed, we had heard of one who had a mind to take a lady's petticoats too and leave her stark naked on the road.

Our carriage came to a halt all of an angle, and Sarah and I clung to each other. We heard Mr Carter shout to someone, employing a good deal of swearing and blaspheming.

'Take heart, my man!' an answering hail came. 'I am not a highwayman. I have merely been assaulted by one.'

'Get out of the way!' Mr Carter swore again and whipped up the horses but (as it turned out) one of our back wheels had gone into a ditch and we did not move an inch.

'I assure you I am speaking the truth!' the man's voice came again. 'I have been abroad and was travelling from Southampton back to my home when I was set upon. My two horses were taken – and my luggage. All I have is what I stand up in.'

'A likely tale!' Mr Carter retorted.

'Indeed not, Sir. I am Giles Copperly and my family lives in Parkshot.'

Sarah's arm gripped mine. 'The *Copperlys* . . .' she said.

I gasped and nodded. Parkshot was a hamlet only a spit away from Chertsey, and we knew of the Copperly family, for they were rich spice merchants and had endowed a stained-glass window at our church.

Sarah put her head out of the carriage window. 'Mr Carter,' she said, 'my sister and I know the Copperly family.'

'Do you indeed?' Mr Carter said stoutly.

'I am sure he . . .' she paused. 'Mr Copperly, what is the name of your father?'

'It is Thomas, Madam,' the answer came.

'That's right.' Sarah opened the carriage door and Giles Copperly strode over. He was about twenty-five and swarthy, with dark eyes and good teeth.

'Your servant, ladies,' he said, bowing very deeply, and I felt that, had he had one, he would have flourished a plumed hat as he made his addresses.

There was a *hurrumph* from Mr Carter. 'If you're sure, Ma'am,' he said.

Sarah nodded her assent to Mr Carter. 'I am Sarah, and this is my sister Hannah,' she said to Giles Copperly. He gave a nod towards me and I smiled and inclined my head slightly, as I had seen the quality do. 'We live at Chertsey and are going home to our family,' Sarah went on. 'We're sorry for your predicament and will be pleased to convey you to Parkshot.'

'Thank the Lord!' said Giles Copperly, and he seized Sarah's hand and kissed it. She looked at him, smiling, and, to my great surprise (for gallants coming into the shop often flirted and it was nothing to us), blushed scarlet.

Mr Carter called for Giles's aid in setting the carriage straight, and (while Sarah, I noticed, was patting her hair and pinching her lips together to make them pink) he helped get it from the ditch and back on to the road. He then joined us for the rest of the journey. While I had hoped for some lively talk – for it turned out that he had just returned from the South Sea Islands – he and Sarah kept most of the conversation between the two of them, and spoke of little but spices and sugars all the way to Parkshot. We left him there, and indeed I was glad to see him go, for I thought him a bore, and we were then driven the short distance home.

We drove through the high street of Chertsey, and – it being rare to see such a beautiful and costly coach-

and-four going through the town – people stopped and stared at us and we, seeing folk we knew, laughed and waved to them. As we drove I was mighty relieved to see that nowhere in the town were there signs of plague: no houses enclosed, no doors with the dread sign on them, and the churchyard stood as tranquil as before, the ground not raised and swollen with bodies as had been the case in London.

Leaning from the coach window, I directed Mr Carter down our lane. Our cottage, cosy and newly thatched with golden straw, stood just beyond the apple orchard, and my brothers were perched on the gate which led into this, playing Jack-come-up and pushing each other from the top bar, as they always did. Suddenly, though, they saw the smart carriage coming towards them and became still as statues, their mouths perfect circles of astonishment.

We just had time to admire our beautiful orchard, alight with white blossom, and the barn where Father worked, which was covered all over with glossy ivy and starry forsythia, before the carriage halted and Mr Carter got down to open the door and lower the carriage steps for us.

Sarah and I exchanged glances and she put her finger against her lips. We lifted our skirts and climbed out in a genteel manner, being sure to keep our faces low so that the boys could not see who we were – but I had reckoned without my hair, and there was no hiding *that*. Before I had even taken a step on to the ground Adam shouted, 'It's Hannah and Sarah!' and all three boys flung themselves on us with squeals and shrieks of laughter. At the noise they made, Anne ran from the cottage, closely followed by Mother, all set to admonish the boys for acting familiarly with two such grand ladies. These two halted on the path and then we had the bigger surprise, for we could see that our mother was expecting a child, and indeed was so very large that it seemed she might produce it at any moment.

She hugged us as close as she was able, and wept, and we wept too, and were glad to be safely home. 'All my children together,' she said, 'gathered in like the harvest.'

Near a week later Sarah and I were ourselves sitting on the orchard gate amid the fast-falling blossom. We had just returned from Abby's cottage, where we'd had to tell her mother how she had died of plague. Although we'd emphasised how brave she'd been, and that it was due to her that the life of little Grace had been saved, it was obvious that Abby's mother would rather have had her own daughter safe and did not care two jots for some other person's child. She had cried, too, because she would have no tranquil churchyard to visit or lay flowers in, Abby's body having gone into a plague pit along with so many others.

'I wish we had taken some memento from Abby,' I said as Sarah and I sat on the gate, talking of what had been said. 'A lock of her hair or some trinket – or at least a word or two from Abby to her mother.'

'There was no time for things like that,' Sarah said. 'We were too anxious to snatch Grace and get away. But mayhap we should have made up some last words to be of comfort to her mother.'

I sighed and nodded, for it had been a difficult and

awkward visit and we'd been only too anxious to leave the poor woman and come home. After some moments I tried to put this sad matter out of my head, however, and looked at Sarah to try to judge her mood, for she'd been acting rather oddly the last day or so. 'When do you think we'll return to London?' I asked.

'You seem in a great hurry.'

I shrugged. 'Well, I thought we agreed we wanted to get our business going again, the shop open and the customers back and . . .'

'And see Tom!' she finished.

'That as well,' I said, my heart giving a little leap.

There was a long pause. 'Hannah, you may not be altogether happy with this, but I think we ought to stay until our mother's lying-in,' Sarah finally said.

'That long!' I protested, for in spite of Mother's girth, there was more than a month to go before our new brother or sister would be born.

'Mother is not so strong as she was for birthing or for the demands of a new baby. We know how hard *that* is from looking after Grace,' Sarah said.

'But Anne will help! And the maid from the village comes in every day.'

'The maid has enough to do with the boys – and Anne is just a lazy flibbertigibbet!'

I laughed, but it was true, for Anne's head was stuffed with games and fashions and fol-de-rols. Further, as she had not bothered overmuch with school, she could barely read or scribe her name.

'She'll be no help at all to our mother!' Sarah said. 'And as we are the eldest daughters, I feel we should stay.'

I sighed. 'But for how long?'

'Eight weeks or so – maybe twelve. We'll see.'

I gave a cry of protest, counting on my fingers. 'Twelve weeks will be July! We'll have lost all our customers by then – they'll have gone elsewhere for their sweetmeats.'

'Tush!' Sarah said. 'There are only a few sweetmeat shops in the west of the City – and we are most certainly the best. They'll come back to us.'

'But . . .' I sighed again, for I could barely explain how much I wanted to go back to London, for I hardly understood it myself. I'd hated the stinking city when we'd left, could hardly bear to think on its name, but now that the plague had disappeared from the streets the people would be back, the theatres and shops would be open and we would find everything as cheery as it had been before. Besides (and this was what I most feared), if I was too long in returning, Tom might find another sweetheart, for there had been no words spoken or pledges given, nor even a kiss.

'Hannah, I think we must stay here a while,' Sarah said gently.

Cross and disgruntled, I jumped down from the gate to go inside, leaving Sarah sitting gazing into the distance. I loved my home and my family, but while I'd been away I'd grown apart from them. Although close in age, I now fancied myself much more mature than Anne, and as for John, George and Adam – well, they drove me quite demented, following me around and putting on my voice until I could scream. Moreover, although Mother was as sweet as she'd always been, Father was often crotchety and preoccupied with his business, seeming none too pleased that he would soon have a new babe in the house. All in all, now the excitement of our return was over and we had told and re-told all our adventures, Chertsey was in every way as tedious as I'd always known it to be.

I went into the cottage and sat at the window seat, staring down the lane. Another twelve weeks! How would I bear it? I could write to Tom, perhaps, care of his master Doctor da Silva to whom he was apprenticed, and tell him that I had not forgotten him and would be returning soon. I had done this once before from Dorchester, but had not had a reply, and indeed I was not sure it had ever reached him, for our letter to Mother and Father had not done so.

As I thought on, my attention was caught by a movement further down the lane. There was a horseman riding towards our cottage, and I knew immediately that it was Giles Copperly, for he'd visited us the day before, and the day before that, each time to thank us for conveying him home. Three visits in a week!

As I watched, he stopped where Sarah was sitting on the gate and jumped from his horse. Sarah took his outstretched hand but, instead of helping her from the gate, he put her hand to his lips and kissed it. They then gazed at each other so long, with the blossom falling all around them, that I was embarrassed and felt obliged to turn away.

It was then that I realised. Of course! *That* was why she did not wish to return to London . . .

The boys were in bed and the candles lit when, that evening, Sarah told Mother she would be staying in

Chertsey to help her through her lying-in.

Mother was so content with this news that it made me feel guilty that I did not really wish to stay. Yet I could not resist a sly dig at Sarah, saying that I had noticed Giles Copperly had called a third time – surely he hadn't wanted to thank us *again* for our trouble?

'No,' she said, blushing. 'No, he merely called to ask if I wished to see the extent of spices they have in their warehouse at Parkshot. I will be visiting there next week.'

Mother, Anne and I looked at her. 'Indeed?' Mother said.

Sarah rose and pretended to tend the fire. 'Yes. They have vanilla, nutmeg, aniseed and a type of cinnamon I've never heard of. Mr Copperly feels we may wish to use some for our sweetmeats.'

'Giles Copperly!' said Mother. That was all, but the way in which she spoke said much.

'He is very handsome. Is he your beau?' Anne asked eagerly, but Sarah did not reply.

'So you two girls will be staying here and eating like horses for another two-month, will you?' Father put in.

I looked at Sarah. 'We will be back in London by the middle of July for definite, won't we?' I asked.

'Of course,' Sarah said. 'Our new babe will be settled in and Mother will be recovered by that time.'

'And mayhap you will have seen enough cinnamon by then,' I teased, and had the satisfaction of seeing her blush again. We sat gazing into the fire and the only sound was the crackle of wood and a *phut-phut* as Father pulled on his pipe of tobacco.

'Hannah,' Anne suddenly piped up. 'If you are so

anxious to get back to London, why don't you go ahead by yourself?'

I looked at her, my heart giving a great leap. Never had Anne said anything so clever.

'You couldn't do that,' Mother said immediately.

'Of course you couldn't,' Sarah said. 'And you couldn't manage to make sweetmeats, run the shop and serve folk all on your own.'

'Well, then!' Anne said. 'What if I went with her? We could do these things between us.' She looked around at everyone beseechingly. 'If I was in London I would work very hard! You would be surprised at how hard I would work.'

I gave a little gasp at this suggestion, but as it did not get shouted down straightaway, began to get fearful excited.

'What do you think, Father?' Mother asked after a moment.

'I think it's a sound idea,' he replied. 'Anne could learn a trade and we would have two less mouths to feed.'

'But do you think Anne could do such a job?' Mother asked Sarah.

'Of course she could,' I put in quickly. 'She could do all the tasks that I used to do: shopping and fetching water from the conduit and grinding down the sugarloaf. She can serve in the shop while I do the skilled work,' I added, for I had already learned much of the trade from Sarah.

'And what would Anne do when you returned to London, Sarah?' Mother asked.

'Well,' Sarah said slowly. 'If things work out with Anne in London I will bide my time here and stay with you a while longer, Mother. Until the babe is weaned, perhaps.'

'And then Anne could come back to Chertsey or we would find her another job in London,' I said, and I spoke joyfully, for in my mind's eye I could already see the reunion of me and Tom – of us meeting and kissing and walking through flowers together, like in the ballad sheets.

'But are you perfectly sure that it's safe?' Mother asked.

'Of course, Mother!' I flew to kiss her. 'London is as safe as houses!'

Chapter Five

London

*'May Day and thence to Westminster, on the way
meeting many milkmaids with their garlands upon
their pails, dancing with a fiddler before them.'*

'What is that great hulking place?'
　'Oh! Who does that forward baggage think she is!'
'Hannah! Look at their gowns!'
'What a beautiful barge!'
'Do look at that!'
As we made our steady progress up the River
Thames, Anne was testing my patience sorely, leaning
first to the left of the open wherry, then to the right,
pointing, exclaiming, gasping and calling for me to
look at first one thing then another. It was May Day
and it seemed that most of London was on the river.

Mother had asked that we stay in Chertsey until
May Day, and on the previous evening she, Sarah,
Anne and I had gone into the orchard as we always
had on this day, and spread linen cloths under the
trees. At dawn we had risen, run into the orchard
(although Mother had not run) and pressed the damp

cloths over our faces and arms, for everyone knew that washing your face in the dawn dew gathered on the first of May was a great beautifier.

Thus refreshed, we had gone home for bread and milk, and then the whole family had walked to the village green where a maypole had been erected and where there was a small May Fair with stalls selling pewter and china and fruit and toys, and sideshows with jugglers, tooth-pullers and dancing milkmaids. Anne and the boys were highly entertained at these, but it was not much to me after the amusements of London – although I did not say as much.

It was a happy farewell to Chertsey, though, for after spending all morning at the fair, Anne and I had walked down to the wharf with our family and caught the boat to London, which was to bring us all the way in four hours. Mother and Sarah had wept as we boarded the craft, but Anne and I had not, for neither of us could contain our excitement at the adventure before us.

We had passed Hampton Court (where the king, it was said, kept two spare mistresses in case he should stay overnight) and also the great palace at Richmond where Good Queen Bess had died. With each mile we covered, the number of craft on the Thames increased until, near the City, a myriad of little boats covered the water from side to side: sculls, skiffs, wherries, decorated rowing boats and the magnificently ornate barges that belonged to the various Guilds of the City.

About two hours into our journey, Anne (who carried two lidded baskets made by our father) said she had a confession to make. I, being in the best of moods, said that I would forgive her, for the day was fair and nothing could be *that* wrong.

She then pulled out the smaller of the baskets, which I had noticed her fiddling with for some time, opening and closing its lid. 'I have brought a friend,' she said, looking at me imploringly, 'for I could not bear to part with her.' Saying this, she lifted the lid and presented me with a white kitten, which she put upon my lap, saying, 'Isn't she pretty? Just look at her pink ears! I could not bear to leave her behind.'

The kitten immediately crawled up to my shoulder and, as she seemed about to make a leap into the river, I took her up and placed her back in the basket, sighing a little. I felt it was fitting that I should sigh, being the older sister and the one in charge, but to tell the truth I loved cats as much as she did and did not mind a bit. Besides, I knew London still had a shortage of animals and that she – and her kittens in time – would be welcome there.

'You're not very cross, are you?' Anne said. 'One of the farm cats had five kittens and I couldn't leave them all behind. I almost brought two—'

'It'll be you who'll look after her,' I warned. 'You must find scraps for her to eat and clean up any messes.'

'Oh, I will!' she said fervently.

'And you must keep her in that basket and not let her out until we reach the shop.'

Some of the bigger craft had musicians, or a fiddler or singer, and these provided entertainment for the passengers who, dressed richly and to be seen, lounged on the decks drinking wine and partaking of food. As we passed Chelsea we came across a skiff containing four rather drunk gallants, and they, seeing us, urged their boatman to follow us upstream. For two miles or so they did so, calling us 'Charmers' and 'Sweet Angels' and sending extravagant compliments across the water, promising not only undying love, but all manner of jewellery and fine things if only we'd join them. We did not deign to even look their way, of course, but there was much giggling between me and Anne and we were rather sorry when, their boatman seeming as drunk as they were, they lost us amid the crush somewhere before the king's palace.

Here, at Whitehall, we had the biggest thrill of all, because the royal barge sailed by us with the king himself on board. His Majesty was seated on an ornately carved chair at the prow, and looked the very image of the man we had seen depicted on news-sheets and inn signs: handsome, strong and lusty. He had olive skin, long black hair which fell curling to his shoulders, and a narrow dark moustache, and was magnificently clothed in satins and lace with a fur-trimmed velvet cape hung about his shoulders. He smiled and waved to those around him, exuding a charm and a presence which drew all eyes. Several spaniels must have been playing about his feet, for we could hear them yapping, and when a barge piled with animal skins passed by, two of them jumped up to a ledge at the stern and hung there, sniffing the air, like tiny figureheads.

His Majesty's barge had lavish ornamentation and was most excellently carved and gilded, with all manner of bright pennants fluttering from its awning. Queen Catherine was quietly seated under a tapestry canopy in the shade (for it was said that she was expecting a child), and looked a neat body, and refined, and on seeing her our eyes raked the area to the back of the barge, hoping we might glimpse Barbara Castlemaine or another of the Ladies of the Bedchamber, but we did not. On board there was a quartet of musicians and all around us on the water people were shouting, 'Long live the King!' and 'God bless His Majesty!' We joined in, shouting, 'A Health to King Charles!' louder than anyone else, for we were fair excited out of our wits to see him there.

Indeed we could not have travelled by river on a better occasion, for there was so much to see that, when Anne was not giddily exclaiming at the sights around us, she was struck speechless at them. I, too, was both awestruck and astounded, but sought to appear more knowing, mindful that I was eighteen months older and had lived in London before.

Passing the great warehouses, tanneries and chandlers along the quayside of the City, our wherry landed at Swan Steps just before London Bridge (at which sight Anne almost collapsed with wonder and astonishment). Here we alighted, which was no easy matter for the landing jetty was slippery-thick with mud and detritus. We had no clogs or pattens to lift us out of the mud, but were wearing leather mules with our best gowns and carrying bundles and bedrolls as well as baskets and the kitten. The waterdog who'd rowed us there came to our aid, however, taking our baggage first and then sweeping us up and throwing us over his shoulder to carry us in turn to the top of the steps. Thus safely landed, I paid our fare and gave a generous tip and, with kitty in the basket meowing piteously, we set off for Crown and King Place and the shop. I was tingling all over now, happy to be back, thrilled at the thought that I'd soon be seeing Tom again.

Anne stopped at the top of Fish Lane. 'Can we go on to the bridge?' she asked breathlessly, looking back at it. 'Just to look . . .'

I shook my head. 'We cannot!' I said. 'Not with all the things we have to carry. See how crowded it is up there! We would be pushed this way and that and robbed of everything we have.'

Anne looked sorely disappointed, so I added that although we ought to get to our shop quickly for the sake of the poor enclosed kitten, we'd return as soon as we could. Our load was such that I was tempted to take a sedan chair, but did not because I had never hailed one before and was not sure of the correct procedure. Besides, it being May Day, some skipjack chair-carrier would be sure to overcharge me, and I had promised Sarah that I would look after the sum of money she'd given me, trade sensibly and not get fleeced.

It was taking an age to get through the crowds for, in spite of the incessant mewling of the kitten, Anne was stopping on every corner to gawp and gaze at the streets, the shops and the passers-by. I thought how different London looked from the way I'd last seen it. Looking now at the hoards of people, the crowded shops, the noisy taverns and the countless street-sellers shouting their wares, it was difficult to picture the City as it had been: bleak and silent, its streets rank with death. It felt to me now as if that other, plague-infested city had been but a dream.

'I never thought there were so many people in the

world,' Anne said wonderingly, as we paused at Cheapside and looked down the wide cobbled street thronging with horses and carriages and people dressed in their best. 'And such things to buy!' she added, darting to a window where all manner of luxurious silk and satin collars and scarves were displayed. 'I swear I will not rest until I have visited every shop in London.'

'Then I fear you will never sleep!' I retorted.

We walked deeper into the City, away from the crowds and through the lanes and alleys. Here I could see traces of the year before, for there were shops still closed and shuttered and houses – once shut-up – which still bore marks of the red cross which had been painted on them, or had their doors still barred. In some of these, whole families had died and no one had come forward to take over the accommodation.

Anne paused before one of the churchyards, looking through the railings curiously. 'Why is the ground raised on each side of the walkway?' she asked. 'It is fully six feet above the path.'

Something caught at my heart and I stood quietly for a moment, for it was this churchyard, St Dominic's, which early on in the plague time had taken the corpses of the four young children who had been neighbours of ours, and their mother as well. 'Because so many died of plague they had no space to bury them all properly,' I explained to Anne. 'They just had to pile bodies upon bodies until they could put in no more. And when the graveyards were full right up they took to throwing corpses into plague pits.'

Anne gasped. 'Bodies upon bodies . . .' she breathed.

'They say one hundred thousand died in all.'

'One hundred thousand!' Anne said wonderingly. 'I do not know and cannot think what that number is.'

'And it is better that you don't,' I said.

We moved on. We were very near our shop now and I began to be nervous, for I had no idea what I'd find. Had all our neighbours perished? Had our shop been looted of what little we had left? Had some drunken hawker, seeing it was empty, set up home in it? Where would I turn for help if things were not as they should be?

'There's our sign!' I said to Anne, pointing above the row of shops to where the metal sign swung and creaked. 'See the sugared plum!'

We reached the shop and stood outside, staring up. The floor above had been rented by a rope-maker who had stored his twines there; but I didn't know whether he had survived the plague or not.

'Is this it, then?' Anne asked, disappointment in her voice, and I remembered that when I'd arrived a year back, I'd been disappointed at the sight of it too. 'It's quite small,' she said.

I nodded. 'I know. It's not like the shops on the bridge – or in Cornhill or Cheapside. Were you expecting more?'

'I thought it would be bigger,' she said. 'Varnished in bright colours. With a glass window.'

'Well, maybe if we work hard and make our fortune we'll be able to have one of those soon. A little shop in the Royal Exchange, perhaps!' I put my bundles on the ground, found the key (which Sarah had placed on a long ribbon around my neck for safekeeping) and opened the shop door. It was dank and gloomy in there, though, and we needed the shutters opened before we could see anything. These, however, were fixed with pegs and a turning device, and a damp winter had swelled them so that they no longer turned. After a struggle I went to the shop of our neighbour, Mr Newbery, who, trading under the sign of the Paper and Quill, sold parchments and fine writing paper.

I pushed open the door of his shop somewhat nervously, for I had last seen Mr Newbery at the very height of the plague when people had been dropping like flies around us. The day Sarah and I had left London he'd informed us he was going to shut up shop and take up drinking at the Two Pigeons instead.

He was back in his shop now, however: a short stocky man bent over the counter reading *The Intelligencer*, his oversized wig pushed to the back of his head. He looked mighty surprised when he saw it was me.

'Young Hannah!' he said. 'How are you? Not dead of the sickness, then?'

'No, indeed not!' I said, smiling to myself as I remembered Mr Newbery's relish for conversation of a morbid nature. 'I am here to open up our shop.'

'Your sister Sarah is with you?'

'No, she—'

'She's dead?'

I laughed. 'No. She is well. I have my younger sister with me – Sarah is staying at home to help our mother with her lying-in.'

'Ah, lying-in,' he said. 'A tricky business. Midwives kill more than they save.'

'Well, it is our mother's seventh and she will more

73

than likely deliver it herself,' I said. 'But I am here to beg your help, Mr Newbery. Our shutters are jammed and we need a man's strength.'

'You're going to start trading again?'

'We are.'

He shook his head, sighing. 'Your rooms are like to be in a terrible state – fair eaten away by rats, I should think. Or dripping damp from the rain we've had over the past months. And to be in London now – don't you know that there have been bad omens about this year? There is a hellfire preacher at St Paul's who says that God's dreadful punishment will be meted out to sinful London soon.'

'But you're still trading,' I pointed out.

'Well, that's as maybe,' he said gruffly, pulling his wig forward on his head and straightening the curls.

He took a small hammer and a stool from beneath his counter, then followed me outside. I presented my sister to him and, after scaring her by telling her about a pamphlet detailing a seer's vision of the City set all in flame from one end to the other, he got up on the stool and tapped on the turning peg with a small hammer to release the shutter. This shutter, when lowered, allowed light into the shop and also formed a counter from which to sell our sweetmeats.

'As I thought – all of a muddle and a mess,' Mr Newbery said with satisfaction, peering into the room and shaking his head.

He went back into his own shop and Anne and I then surveyed the room before us, which was not much spoiled – although the walls were mould-ridden and would need washing, and the herbs we'd strewn on the floor were black and gave off a musty, unpleasant smell. The fireplace was laid neat and tidy, however, with the fire irons all in place and the saucepans set above, and there was the small burner to heat the sugar water nearby. To one side of the room was the marble working surface on which stood various sizes of wooden drums. These were empty and dusty now but, after a visit to the market, would soon contain sugar, spices and the various fruits and herbs with which we worked.

'It is a good business, and we must work hard and make a success of what we do, for Sarah's sake,' I said to Anne.

'Of course we will!' My sister took Kitty (for thus we had named her) from her basket and began to walk around the shop with her, and then into the living quarters beyond, telling her that this would be her new home and she wasn't to stray but must stay with us and be a good, playful kitty.

'Anne, are you listening?' I asked.

She nodded. 'You said we must work hard.' She put Kitty down and turned to me, looking puzzled. 'But what was that that your neighbour was saying – about the City in flame?'

'It was nothing,' I said. 'Mr Newbery likes to scare.'

And if God's dreadful punishment was being meted out to the City, I thought to myself, then surely it had happened last year. The plague. Nothing could be worse than that.

It is well known that a London housewife may buy everything she needs from her own doorstep, and we proved this by setting our shop to rights without needing to go abroad for any of our purchases. Within two days the walls – both in the shop and our room beyond – were newly limewashed, the floor was scrubbed with soda and strewn with fresh herbs, and a new water carrier and some enamel jugs had been purchased. There were fresh wax candles in all the holders and two shimmering sugar loaves standing ready to be used. Thus all was prepared, and it just remained for us to go to Covent Garden market to buy the blooms and the fruits we needed to start making the sweetmeats.

Before I'd left Chertsey, Sarah and I had talked about what should be made first, and had decided upon frosted rose petals, orange and lemon suckets and herb comfits. These were simple sweetmeats which Anne could help with and which we knew sold well. Once we had a few regular sweetmeats in stock, we would then begin to make the more time-consuming things: the marchpane fruits, the crystallised violets and the sugared plums.

All was prepared, then, and I was mighty pleased with myself. There was one thing I had not done, though, and it was on my mind constantly. I had not yet been to Doctor da Silva's to speak to Tom.

We were too busy, I told myself, there was much to put to rights, and I could not leave Anne, for she needed to be instructed all along the way. These were my excuses – but what truly delayed me was the thought that Tom might have forgotten about me in the eight months that I'd been gone – for it was said that 'prentices bedded where they could, and why should he wait for a girl who might not ever return to him? Moreover, a girl he had not even kissed. All the while I did not go to see him, then, I could pretend that all was well between us.

Late on the afternoon of our third day there, however, all being done in the shop, the part of me that wanted to see Tom won over the part that was afeared, and on an impulse I took off my work clothes and put on my best green taffeta gown, which I had worn all that time ago when Tom and I had walked to Chelsea to pick violets, and which I'd left in our back room. I caught up my hair in a top-knot, as was now the fashion in London, and put some sprigs of deep blue rosemary flowers into my curls. Rosemary for remembrance, I thought, and prayed that I had not slipped far from his mind.

Before I left I circled the shop, swirling my skirts around to show the darker green lining and ruffled underskirt. 'Do I look very fine?' I asked Anne. 'Do you think my Tom will be fair overcome at the sight of me?'

She laughed and nodded. 'But you must pull your bodice down a little to show more of what a man likes to see!'

I pretended to look shocked. 'You have been learning such things from the minxes in our village, I suppose.' Anne blushed and I added, 'I am quite confident of Tom's good opinion without doing that, thank you kindly.' (Although truth may have it that I did go into our room and lace my bodice a little tighter, which had more or less the same effect.)

Going up the lane towards Doctor da Silva's shop I felt both excited and nervous. I would not take for granted that we were sweethearts, I decided, but would act as if I were someone recently returned from the country calling on an old friend.

As I rounded the corner I saw, glinting, the sign of the Silver Globe hanging outside the apothecary's shop, and my heart caught in my throat. How often over the past months had I dreamed of coming back here and seeing Tom, of him looking up and seeing me standing there, then coming to me and taking my hand . . .

But . . . but when I reached the shop the windows were shuttered, the door was barred with two planks of wood across it and – oh, foul thing! – a faded red cross was upon the door.

Plague!

My heart began beating loudly – so loudly that I could hear it in spite of the noise all around. I stood quite still for some moments, trying to control this, and then I began to walk around the shop examining the shuttered windows in case there was a crack I could see through. There was not, however, and I came once more to the door and stood before it, pressing my hands against the wood as if it could impart some secret to me. I closed my eyes and saw again the shop as it had been last September: windows full of plague preventatives and a trail of people outside, some with plague tokens on them, some with discharging buboes, all waiting to see Doctor da Silva and be treated, for many physicians had already left the City and the poorer folk had nowhere else to go. It should be no surprise to me that he and Tom had succumbed to the disease. Why had I thought that they had some special immunity?

Behind me I heard a street-hawker's cry of 'Hot faggots! Five for sixpence!', but I did not turn.

'You want an apothecary, dearie?'

I opened my eyes and an old woman was looking up at me, bent low under the burden of a tray of faggots which she carried tied around her neck.

I shook my head. 'I don't want an apothecary – well, I do, but only this one.'

'Doctor da Silva? He stayed to help us, didn't he? Poor man. He went the way of most of 'em that stayed. He and his lad both.'

'They . . . they both contracted plague?'

'Aye,' she nodded, swaying on the stick. 'They was taken ill just when we was athinking it was all over. Near Christmas, it was.'

'Do . . . do you remember what happened?'

She shrugged. 'What happened? Only the usual thing: one day they was here, the next they was poorly, the next they was dead.'

'They are . . . truly dead, then?' I asked.

'Aye. Both of 'em. Dead and in the pit. I kept indoors most of that time meself. Didn't go out for three months and near starved.' She suddenly gave me a suspicious look. 'But why do you need a 'pothecary? Do you have a fever?'

I shook my head.

'They say plague may return if we don't take care.'

I didn't speak.

'I keep three spiders in my pocket whenever I go aselling faggots. What do you do?'

But I couldn't reply to this for my throat was thick with tears and I felt near choked with them. After a moment she moved on, looking at me strangely. 'Five for sixpence! Five faggots for sixpence!' she called as she moved down the lane.

I stayed leaning against the shop front for some

time, tears falling down my cheeks and marking the green taffeta gown. And then I pulled the rosemary sprigs out of my hair and let them fall, for there was no one here to remember me.

Chapter Six

Nelly Gwyn

'Saw pretty Nelly standing at her lodgings door in Drury Lane in her smock-sleeves and bodice – she seemed a mighty pretty creature.'

Anne did not find me good company in those days after I had first learned of Tom's death for, being full of sorrow, I made a hard task-mistress. Not sleeping well, I rose before dawn, worked all day and continued toiling by the light of a candle at night, and expected her to do the same.

I found it hard to believe that I had lost Tom for ever. With my friend Abby I had seen her grow weaker and more pitiful, day by day as the plague took a tighter grip on her. That she would die had seemed inevitable. Tom, though . . . the last I'd seen of him he had been strong and healthy and brave, blowing kisses to me as our carriage had driven away from London. How could he be dead?

I lay awake at night with Anne sleeping peacefully beside me, and couldn't help wondering in which way he had been struck down. I had seen or heard of plague taking many forms: brief and so violent that the sufferers were dead before they knew they had contracted it; painful but drawn out over a long, weary period so that they almost believed they might survive; or so prolonged and maddening in its intensity that the victims dashed their brains out against a wall in order to find peace.

Which had Tom endured?

I knew again, too, the sorrow of not having a grave to visit. After our grandmother in Chertsey had died we would go to the churchyard several times a year to take flowers or – on her birthday – to decorate the grave with cut-out pictures and black ribbons. I would have felt greatly comforted if I could have visited Tom's grave, for I would have taken paper love-hearts as well as flowers, and sat and told him what was in my heart. There was nowhere to go, though, no grassy mound to sit beside, and although I made enquiries at the parish church, they told me that on contracting plague he and Doctor da Silva had been taken to a pesthouse in another parish. On asking there, I was told they had died and their bodies tipped into a plague pit. It was not even known which pit it was, except that it had been outside the City walls.

After two weeks of continual moping my dark mood was arrested, however, by Anne's announcement that she wanted to go back to Chertsey.

We had just shut the shop and I had put her to grinding down sugar for the next day's sweetmeats, hardly noticing that she was tired and unhappy.

'Hannah,' she suddenly announced. 'You're not the same sister that I remember. You're miserable and hag-ridden and I declare I want to go home.'

I could scarce believe my ears. 'Why, what are you saying?'

'I know you've lost your sweetheart, and I've held my tongue thinking you would get over your bad humour, but it looks to be getting worse and you're more miserable by the minute,' she said defiantly. 'I'd thought we'd have a rare old time here in London and enjoy each other's company and be going to fairs and plays and suchlike, but all I do is grind sugar day and night – and moreover, be held up to ridicule for not doing it well enough!'

I stared at her in surprise, for this speech was so unlike Anne that I could only think that she had been rehearsing it for days.

'So if you'll pay me my wages to date I'll take Kitty and make my own way home,' she continued, 'for I'd rather stay in Chertsey with the heifers than be in London with a shrew!'

'Oh!' I gasped.

'So there. I've said it and am glad on it.'

I looked at my little sister standing there so defiantly and, although I was very much hurt, recognised more than a little of the truth in what she'd said.

'A shrew, you say . . .'

'I didn't mean that last bit.'

'Yes, you did!'

'Well. Only sometimes.'

There was a long pause. 'Am I really so bad?' I asked.

She nodded. 'I can never speak to you. You're always miserable. You stand and watch everything I do and then say it's wrong.' Her bottom lip trembled. 'I don't like it here now!'

I felt so ashamed at these last words that I went over and put my arms around Anne. 'I'm sorry,' I said. 'I've thought of no one but myself and I've been horrible and beastly.'

'Indeed you have.'

'But please don't go home,' I said, hugging her tightly, 'for I couldn't manage without you.'

'Well,' she said. 'You must promise to be nicer to me, and if you are, perhaps I'll stay . . .'

So we became friends again and I resolved to myself that I would put Tom out of my mind as much as I could, for I knew that everyone had lost someone in the plague: parent, employer, friend, husband, child . . . and if we all went around in low mood and foul temper, then the world would become an awful place indeed.

I began to see another side of Anne, a London side, for here she became a quick and neat worker and not at all lazy. As the weeks went by and the markets became fully open across the City, I allowed her to go off on her own in the mornings to buy the fruit and flowers we needed. She was good at this, for she drove a hard bargain with the stall-holders and, unlike me, was bold enough to return a bloom she later found to be damaged or an orange with a worm at its centre. I did not allow her to handle money, however, for on the two occasions when she had gone out with a pocket of coins under her petticoats, once she had been rooked of all she had by a fortune teller in a booth, and once she had purchased a whistling wooden bird to amuse Kitty, which had broken within the hour. After this I sent her out with trading tokens, or she went to one of our regular suppliers where we had an account.

We spoke often of our family, and whether Sarah and Giles loved each other, and also if our mother had been confined safely and whether we had a new brother or sister. I felt that things had gone all right for our mother, for Sarah would have found means to let us know if this were not the case.

It had been feared that with the coming of warmer weather the plague would return, but although there were always a few plague deaths on the Bills of Mortality, thanks be the numbers did not increase. People continued to pour into London – either returning to their old jobs or coming to fill up the places left by those who had died – until the City seemed just as crowded and heated and hectic as it had done the previous year.

In the first days after our return we did not have many customers, but we didn't mind this because we didn't have a deal of sweetmeats prepared. By the month of June, however, many of our old customers had realised we were open again and custom began to improve. I was pleased to be in such a trade as ours, for although it is true that sweetmeats are only passing trivial things, our customers held that they made them feel better and cheered their day. One grand lady said to us that if she wanted some sweet delicacy and could afford it, then she would have it, for life was too short to do without.

One day, we made an excursion to see the shops on

London Bridge. It took us fully one hour to fight our way across to Southwarke, for there were forty shops open on the bridge, and as many stalls, and a press of people on foot, horseback, carriage and sedan fighting with each other for space. Here we purchased two pairs of scented gloves each, and a set of nutcrackers at a new cook shop, for one of our most popular sweetmeats was miniature fruits made from marchpane, which meant two or three nights sitting cracking a deal of almonds with a hammer, and the nutcrackers would greatly speed this work.

Leaving the bridge to go around the myriad of little shops near the Tower, we heard a terrible roaring coming from the king's menagerie, making me jump mightily and Anne shriek with fright. We were told by a garlic-seller that it was feeding time for the king's lions and tigers and, hearing this, I promised Anne that we would visit the menagerie soon and see these lions, for they were said to be most enormous and fiercesome, yet related to our own Kitty (which I could scarce believe).

Another day, obtaining some lengths of parchment from Mr Newbery (who asked me if I wanted it to write my Will and said it was wise to do so), I wrote a list of all the sweetmeats that we made, to be advertisements for our goods. This read:

Frosted rose petals
Crystallised violets
Sugared plums
Herb comfits
Sugared angelica
Glacé cherries

Sugared orange peel
Lemon and orange suckets
Violet cakes

As well as these we made the marchpane fruits, of course, but as they took a monstrous long time to make, we could not always hold them in stock. I took great pains with the spellings of these items, even though many of our customers would not have known any better and, after getting some coloured inks from Mr Newbery, drew a likeness of the sweetmeat next to its name for those who could not read. I made two copies and nailed one to the wooden shutter to be on show when we were open, and put the other inside on the wall.

We also began to make pomanders as Martha had instructed us, for at a warehouse in Wharf Lane I'd seen a barrel of cloves going very cheaply and had made bold to buy the lot. Oranges were costly, but we did not need the best quality, nor the freshest, so we would buy five or six of a lesser quality at a time, stud them all over with cloves and decorate them with ribbons and lace. Anne was especially good at doing this and would search around the rag markets for scraps of braid or gay trimmings to use. We hung these pomanders in the shop and they did not stay long, for pretty items like this were much in demand with the quality.

I wanted Sarah to see what a success we were making of things, and looked forward to her return so that we could hear how our mother had fared, yet loved what I was doing so much that I did not want to relinquish my place as shopkeeper. I knew, too, that

Anne would not now wish to return home to Chertsey, so began to wonder if the three of us could work together when Sarah arrived. The shop and the living quarters were small, but Anne could have a truckle bed to pull out from under the bigger one, and perhaps a storeroom could be built at the back of the shop, beside the privy.

Anne and I soon became best friends again, for being very near in age we had always played together as children, and it didn't take long for us to regain our old closeness. Things were going mighty well for us and I would have been happy had it not been for the loss of Tom. Though I did not speak on it now, his memory was always at the back of my mind. I wondered if I would find another sweetheart, and when, and what he would be like. Whenever I daydreamed and thought on this mysterious person, though, he always turned out to have Tom's face. Maybe, I thought, there would be no other suitor for me, and I would remain unkissed and die a spinster.

One morning, to my great surprise, a handsome gilded carriage stopped outside the shop drawn by two white horses with their manes and tails plaited with red and gold ribbons. A velvet-coated footman then jumped down, opened the door with a flourish and lowered the steps.

As I hurried to the doorway to greet this important customer, there was some giggling within the carriage (for it seemed that there was a man in there too), and then a young woman with hair as red as mine stepped out.

I brushed down my apron and just had time to call

Anne to come through from the back room. 'Quickly!' I shouted in great excitement, for I had never forgotten her coming to the shop before. ''Tis Nelly Gwyn. The actress!'

Anne came running in and we both curtseyed to Nelly for, as Mr Newbery said later, although she was but a whore she was a mighty pretty one. She was dressed very beautifully: her gown was of the finest silver tissue and over it she wore a most fashionable little cape of black velvet backed with silver fur.

'I'm pleased to see your shop open again at last!' she said. 'I have oft fancied some of your sweetmeats.'

'Thank you, Ma'am,' I murmured. 'We have but recently returned from the country.'

'And all's well and you have survived the visitation?' She looked through to the back of the shop. 'Where is your sister?'

'She is staying with our family at present, Ma'am,' I said. 'But I have my younger sister here instead.'

Nelly laughed and showed little pearly teeth, perfectly spaced. 'So! A goodly supply of sisters.' She looked around. 'Your shop here is a little oasis. London roars outside as wild as a lion, but in here all is sweetness and calm.'

'Thank you, indeed,' I said, bobbing another curtsey and thinking I would write to Sarah on the instant and tell her this.

'And now will you let me have some of your crystallised violets, for I swear nothing revives me after a performance as they do.'

I was instantly filled with remorse, for we had not been able to find fresh violets at the flower markets in the last week and so did not have any crystallised ones to sell. I apologised for this, and, promising that we would have some by the middle of the following week, persuaded her that lemon suckets might be the very thing to refresh her instead.

I counted ten of these into a large cone of paper. 'Are you on stage at present, Ma'am?' I asked, for I could see from Anne's face that she was struck dumb with admiration and would want to know more about our visitor.

She nodded. 'I am engaged to play Lady Wealthy in *The English Monsieur*. Me – a lady! The very thought has put the aristocracy into a fearsome stir!'

Anne and I both laughed.

Kitty wandered in from our back room and Nelly bent down to pick her up and kiss her, saying, 'I have a fur muff of exactly this colour!' Kitty gave a yowl of protest at being handled, for she was not a cuddlesome cat, and Nelly put her down again. 'Oh – are those oranges?' she exclaimed, pointing at two decorated pomanders which hung in the shop. We said they were, and were for hanging in closets, and Nelly said that until recently she had been selling them in their natural state during the interval at the theatre (which I knew, of course, but affected not to) and would take them both because they were so pretty.

'But have you been to the theatre – either of you?' she asked when she had paid us.

'Never,' I said.

'I have always wanted to!' Anne blurted out.

'Then you shall go.' Twirling a red curl around her finger, Nelly said, 'When I return for my violets I shall bring you tickets for next week's performance.'

We, quite overcome, gave our thanks and curtseyed

again – indeed we were bobbing up and down like ships at sea as she went out. By this time, a small crowd had gathered outside our shop, for Nelly was very popular with the people on account of her having risen from such humble beginnings to this position of prominence. Moreover, it was the talk of the coffee houses (so Mr Newbery informed us) that the king, tiring of Barbara Castlemaine, might take Nelly for his mistress, for he had been seen at the theatre on many occasions when she was performing.

True to her word, Nelly did return for the violets and gave us tickets for the theatre, and Anne and I were both monstrous excited at the thought of going, in spite of Mr Newbery telling us that he would not attend a theatre for a king's ransom. 'They are nasty, crowded places and breeding grounds for all sorts of diseases,' he said.

'Then are not taverns those things, too?' I asked nicely, for Mr Newbery was exceedingly fond of alehouses and was often brought home hung about the shoulders of the night watchman. He did not reply to this.

On the day of the play we shut the shop at midday and were at the theatre for two o'clock, for although the performance did not start before three, we wanted to be sure to see everything there was to be seen. We were dressed in our best – I wearing the plum linsey-woolsey suit which I had made and embroidered, and Anne wearing my blue linen gown of the previous year; we both had new starched lace caps and scented gloves.

The King's Theatre was in Rider's Yard in Drury

Lane, which was a goodly way for us across the City and outside the walls. From the road it looked just like an ordinary building in some disrepair, but inside it had a glass roof and was circular in form, filled by boxes separated from each other and divided into rows going upwards. Our seats were in the middle of the theatre and there was a gallery below us and one above, this latter being where the 'prentices sat. At the bottom was a sloping pit area containing benches where well-dressed young men were sitting, and next to the stage lounged the pretty orange and lemon sellers shouting their wares to the quality and, I noticed, casting their eyes upon the young men nearby as they did so.

Anne and I sat down and began staring avidly at the people there, looking this way and that and exclaiming and gasping by turn. Early though we were, the place was already crowded and noisy with laughter and conversation. People were walking about, changing seats, hailing friends, eating pastries and indulging in horseplay, so that it seemed to me more tavern than theatre.

On stage, acts came and went to amuse the audience before the play began: a dancing bear, a juggler, a man playing a pipe and dancing a jig. No one seemed to take much notice of them. At one point, the 'prentice boys on high started a chant of, 'Nel-ly, Nel-ly! Nel-ly!', which the other men took up, causing us to put our hands over our ears until their yelling ceased.

Anne drew my attention to the pit, pointing out that there were a dozen women sitting with the young gallants. Such women, though! In butterfly colours, they flirted and giggled and moved from one man to another, either wearing glittering masks held to their faces on sticks, or so many patches and sequins that you could scarce see their complexions beneath. Their gowns were of rich materials in delectable colours, but seemed to have been made when they were a deal smaller, for their bosoms looked about to fall out of their bodices.

'They're the whores,' I said, leaning over to whisper in Anne's ear. 'They're looking for business.'

Anne gasped and we both watched, fascinated, for none of the women had the least shame about them, nor looked downcast, but instead lorded it over the men with as many airs and graces as if they were duchesses rather than doxies.

''T'would never do for Chertsey!' Anne said, and we could scarce stop laughing.

It was at this time, just before the play started, that there came on to the stage a man all dressed in black wheeling a large box which he set up on its end. Shouting to be heard above the hubbub, he announced in a strange accent that he was a magician and necromancer by the name of Count de'Ath, and he had brought with him his mysterious cabinet.

A little hush came across the audience, for everyone loved to hear of magic and enchantment (and indeed Anne and I intended to pay a visit to Madame le Strange, the fortune teller on London Bridge, for it was said that she had predicted the plague and foretold the exact number who would die).

Count de'Ath stood full square before the audience, twirled his moustache and said that if any member of the audience wished to disappear, either from his wife or his creditors, then he had only to enter this cabinet and he would never be seen again.

'Where will he go, Maestro?' someone asked from above, and the Count said that the cabinet would instantly convey this man to a land across the sea, where he would live as a person of wealth and property.

''Is troubles vill disappear and he vill for ever dwell in a place of warmth and luxury.'

'I dwells there after five pints at the alehouse!' some wit shouted.

Count de'Ath did not appear to hear this. Indeed, he seemed oblivious to all that was going on in the theatre: the people constantly arriving, the yapping from the lap dogs of the ladies, a brawl taking place in the gallery, a new cry of 'Nel-ly!' beginning from a box.

'How much will it cost to go there?' someone wanted to know.

The Count raised his arms. 'No money vill exchange hands,' he said. There was a pause. 'It vill merely cost 'is soul.'

There was quiet at this, and several people in the audience crossed themselves. Even the harlots stopped their chatter for a moment.

'Are zere any takers?' asked Count de'Ath, but of course there were not, because reading the almanacs and visiting a fortune teller was one thing, but selling your soul to the Devil was quite another.

The Count asked again, telling of how a person's life could be changed, how a man could become a king and live on a rich island of his own for the whole of his life. Suddenly, then, from one of the benches in the pit, a young man stepped forward and ran up the steps on to the stage. He was tall and slim, dressed like a dandy in satins and lace. 'I'll go!' he said, sweeping his feathered hat from his head with a flourish.

Those in the audience who were watching the act started in surprise and then strained forward in their seats in order to see better, while others gasped at his bravery. I gasped loudest of all – indeed I gave a little cry – for as the young man turned, I saw that it was Tom.

Chapter Seven

The Magician

'My wife and I to the theatre where sat the King, Madam Castlemaine, the Duke and Duchess, and my wife to her great content had her full sight of them all.'

Or was it? Just as the young man turned and walked across the stage to enter the black cabinet, a couple pushed past us to their seats and we had to rise. As we sat down another couple came by, laughing, and made to engage us in conversation.

'Damned fine play, this!' said the man. 'Saw it yesterday, too.'

'Have you seen it before?' the woman asked me.

I didn't reply and, stifling a cry, almost pushed them out of the way so I could see around the woman's ribboned cap. They passed by, looking at me curiously and muttering about my rudeness, but it was too late by then, for the young man was inside the cabinet, his face shrouded by darkness.

'What is it?' Anne asked in a whisper as the couple went on. 'Was she a whore too? Is that why you didn't speak to her?'

I shook my head but was not able to explain, for I was rapt, breathless, watching the stage.

Count de'Ath bowed. From the musicians standing by the stage there came a fanfare. 'If any person vants to examine my cabinet, he vill discover no openings or false doors, and no secret passages vere a man might hide!'

'So where is that man going to go?' someone shouted.

'He vill disappear . . . be changed into air and shadow . . . become a ghost creature who vill travel o'er vast continents until he arrives at the land I have pledged. Only then vill he regain his right shape and substance and become a man again!'

There was quite a stir in the audience at this.

Count de'Ath swirled his cloak around to half hide his face. 'I am trained in the black arts and 'ave studied at the hands of demons! Only through me can zis enchantment be achieved.' He paused. 'And just for the price of a soul!' he added.

There was another gasp at this and two gallants arrived on stage to examine the cabinet. Pronouncing it to be in no way out of the ordinary, there was another fanfare and a black curtain was pulled across the front of the box, obscuring the young man within completely from view. The Count made various strange movements over the box, there was the tinkling of bells and a puff of smoke, then the curtain was pulled open.

It was empty. The man inside – whoever he was – had disappeared.

Some people in the audience cried out in

astonishment. The same two gallants then examined the cabinet again and, looking puzzled, pronounced that the young man had gone and they knew not where.

Count de'Ath regarded the audience with some disdain, then gave a short bow before tipping his cabinet on to its side and wheeling it out again without another word. Some people clapped, the 'prentices cat-called, but for the most part those that had watched the performance sat in awed silence.

Anne, too, was spellbound, staring open-mouthed at the stage. 'A real magician. An enchanter.'

'It seems like it,' I said, stunned.

'I've never seen real magic before . . .'

Slowly my heart stopped pounding and regained its normal beat. It couldn't have been Tom – of course it couldn't. The youth on stage had been taller, thinner, the shape of his head had been different.

And Tom was dead, I told myself sternly. No magic on earth could bring him back again. And yet . . . and yet . . .

More entertainment arrived on stage – a man playing the bagpipes – and ten minutes later the play began, although this did not seem to make a jot of difference to the audience. They continued to walk and talk amongst themselves, calling out to compliment or jeer at the actors and actresses. The plot made no sense to me, for I was still stunned by the performance of Count de'Ath, but this did not spoil my enjoyment at being there. When Nelly came on the audience went wild, and indeed she played solely to them, calling, waving and once even neglecting her part on stage to address someone in the pit. At one time she was disguised as a boy (wearing short breeches and showing her legs, which were very slim and shapely) and when she appeared thus the whole audience rose to her, applauding wildly.

At half-time the orange girls came round selling their wares. One sold sweetmeats, too, and we purchased two lemon suckets and were pleased to find that these were inferior to ours and looked rather limp and stale. On tasting, we discovered that they were not so succulent, either, and we decided that they could not have undergone the six days alternately steeping and boiling in sugar water as ours did, but had been made by a quicker and inferior process.

People came round at this time selling ballad sheets and pamphlets, and holding up bills showing what the following week's performances were going to be, and there was also more entertainment on stage, although not Count de'Ath again.

A few moments after the play restarted there came some noises and barking from the royal box above us, and a stir of anticipation ran around the theatre. The barking, it was whispered, was from a pack of spaniels and meant that the king had arrived.

Anne and I were fearful excited at this.

'Again the king!' Anne said, for we often spoke about how we'd seen him in the royal barge, and how neither our mother nor father nor our brothers had ever glimpsed him nor were likely to. 'Today is the best day of my life!' she went on, clasping my hand. 'I will not sleep a wink tonight for the thrill of it all.'

And now no one was watching the stage, for all eyes were fixed on the royal box, and even Nelly had to take second place to His Majesty. News quickly ran round the theatre of what the king was wearing, what humour he was in, and what mistress accompanied him, and Anne and I practically fell out of our seats trying to crane our heads outwards and backwards to obtain information on these subjects for ourselves. Unfortunately, though, the royal box was stuffed with ladies and courtiers who were fawning about His Majesty and keeping him from our view, and we caught no more than brief glimpses of piled, curled hair, gaily-coloured dresses and waving plumed fans. We could not even see which royal mistress he had favoured that day, although were told by someone in front of us that it was not Barbara Castlemaine, but a girl called Mall Davis who was but sixteen.

When the play was over and the king had left, Anne was anxious to go round to the stage door to mingle with the gallants and fops gathered there for a sight of Nelly. I agreed to do this, but only because I had a mind to say a word to Count de'Ath.

The crowd outside the stage door had just set up a cry for Nelly when the Count came out and began to push his way through them. He was dressed in the swirling cloak he had worn on stage, and a black velvet hood lined with crimson.

'Count de'Ath!' I hailed him and, when he turned, called quickly, 'Can you tell me where that young man in your cabinet has gone?'

He looked at me through narrowed eyes. 'Did you not pay heed to what I said? 'E has gone to a new life, Mamzelle. A better life.'

'And can I go there too?' I blurted out, and Anne started and gasped.

'If you enter my cabinet. Come to Bartholomew

Fair!' he said, and then he disappeared beyond the crowd and out of view.

'Why did you say that?' Anne asked, astonished. 'What are you thinking of?'

'I didn't mean it,' I said. 'It was something to say. I was jesting.'

Of course I had been jesting. And besides, it had not been Tom who had been on that stage and had been transported by magic to another place. Whatever conjuring Count de'Ath could do, he could not conjure with someone who was dead.

This did not stop me from daydreaming, however, and on falling asleep that night I could not but think how terrible it would be if Tom had somehow survived the plague only to have been magicked away from me into Count de'Ath's cabinet, and lost his soul . . .

'Wherever did you get those?' I looked at Anne and burst out laughing. I'd sent her to the conduit for water and she'd been gone an age. When she'd come back, her face was stuck all over with black and sequined patches: a heart on her forehead, clubs and spades on her cheeks, a ladybird on her chin.

'Do they look fine?' Anne said, taking up a looking-glass and admiring herself. 'Do I look a lady?'

'You look a harlot!' I said.

'But everyone wears them now!'

'Not shop-girls,' I said, shaking my head. 'How much did you pay for them?'

'I traded a pomander with a woman who runs a stall in Cornhill.' She picked up Kitty, who looked at her in some surprise and then began to pat at her face, no doubt thinking that the face patches were black beetles.

'I have one for you, too,' Anne said to me. 'It is of a miniature coach and horses and you may wear it across your forehead. The woman said that she sold a Countess one just the same.'

'I would sooner have my freckles!' I said.

But Anne thought her patches mighty fine and wore them for the rest of the day – and the next, too, until I thought I'd have to peel them off when she was asleep to be rid of them. She wore them until Mr Newbery came in to impart some tidbit of scandal and, seeing Anne's face, stepped back, looking aghast.

'Have you the pox, Madam?' he asked.

'No, indeed I have not,' Anne said indignantly.

'But the women who wear patches are mostly raddled old bawds who wear them to hide their sores and scars,' he said, and for once I was glad of his dismal perspective, for even before he had finished speaking, Anne had begun peeling them off.

Mr Newbery gave us the gossip, which was that the king's new mistress, Mall Davis, was an actress, and that Nelly Gwyn was so jealous of her that she'd had a song written which poked fun at her rival's legs, which by all accounts were fat and not nearly so elegant as her own. We laughed and said we were on Nelly's side, and then just as Mr Newbery was leaving I suddenly remembered. 'What is Bartholomew Fair?' I asked him. 'And when is it?'

'Bart's Fair?' he asked, scratching his bald head under his wig. 'Why, 'tis a monstrous big fair held on the grounds in Smithfield, by St Bartholomew's hospital. 'Tis there for two weeks at every end of August.'

Anne had gone through to our back room now. She was having trouble removing some of the patches, for they had set hard on her skin, and every now and then she gave a little shriek as she pulled at them.

'And are there conjurers at this fair, and magic men?' I asked him more quietly, for I did not wish Anne to hear.

'There is everything there!' said Mr Newbery. 'Plays and players, dancing shows, educated apes, puppets and horses dancing jigs! The whole world is there.'

I felt excited already. 'Then Anne and I must go!'

Mr Newbery frowned. 'You'll get your throats cut and lose your pockets as sure as a sow drags its belly on the ground!' he said. 'The place is fair bursting with higglers, hawkers and robbers.'

I could not but laugh. 'It's a wonder we've survived in London so long,' I said, 'and thank you for warning me, but I think we'll take our chances. You have painted too exciting a picture for us to miss it.'

Chapter Eight

Bartholomew Fair

'Carried my wife by coach to Bartholomew Fair and showed her the monkies dancing on the ropes. There was also a horse with hoofs curled like Ram's horns, a goose with four feet and a cock with three. Then to see some clockworks and several scripture stories, but above all there was shown the sea, with Neptune, Venus, mermaids and the sea rolling.'

As soon as we came to Smithfield market, which led on to the fair, I began to be afeared that I would lose Anne, for seeing the field set with such a gay scene stretching in all directions she began uttering little shrieks of excitement and running here, there and everywhere, so that I wished I had her on a restraining tether like a child. As Mr Newbery had said, it was a monstrous big fair and would likely take several days to get around it all.

By Smithfield, forty roast pigs turned on their spits as the butchers cried up their products. There was a rich smell in the air, the sizzle of crackling and the singe of smoke. 'Tender pork! Here's your delicate pig and pork!' they called. 'A good sausage, and well made!'

'Hot sheep's feet!'

'Rare beefsteaks!'

'Trotters all hot!'

I stopped to sniff the tantalising odours, suddenly feeling hungry.

'What d'you lack, sweet ladies? What d'you lack?'

Two peddlers stopped before us, their trays laden with an assortment of braids and tassels, ribbons and silk flowers.

'Oh, what lovely colours!' Anne said, straightaway delving into a tangled skein of ribbons.

'Fine ribbons, pin cases, lovely flowers – what d'you lack?'

'We lack nothing at the moment,' I said to them, pulling Anne's hand away. 'For we have just arrived and must see everything else before we buy.' But we had made the mistake of pausing and looking, and now found ourselves surrounded by a dozen or more hawkers.

'Fine pears!' one called.

'Sweet gingerbread!'

'Ballads, fine new ballads!'

'Fresh fish . . . fresh new fish!'

'Fine singing birds!'

'Ink – seven pence a pint! Very fine, bright ink!'

'Strawberries ripe! Cherries! Asparagus!'

'A powder for a flea!'

A crowd of them were round us, and indeed it seemed that every London peddler and street seller was today at Bartholomew Fair trying to do business.

I grasped Anne's hand. 'Come and we will run for it!' I said to her and, dodging through the sellers, we ran across the grass towards the bigger booths and the striped tents and awnings, all bright with fluttering flags and streamers.

Pausing by a puppet show, I spoke to Anne seriously. 'You must show no interest in buying anything,' I said, 'or you will find we have spent our money before we have even started. You must stay beside me all the time, and not go wandering off. And you must keep your hand on your pocket all the time, for everyone has told us of the cut-purses here and Mr Newbery seems to think that we'll be lucky enough to get home with our heads on.'

'But it's all so thrilling!' she said breathlessly. 'And I've never before seen such sights in all my life. Nor so many of them!'

I could not but smile. 'Neither have I. But we must be cautious,' I added.

Arm in arm we began to stroll through the tents and booths, admiring, exclaiming and gasping by turn and not knowing what our eyes would fall on next. There were rare sights to see, and the dress and appearance of the visitors (who were of the quality as well as tag, rag and bobtail) were almost a show of their own. The ladies were dressed in their best, but it was a mixed best: some wearing full wigs, face masks and vast plumed hats, some up from the country in out-of-fashion moiré dresses with straw bonnets, some in neat riding habits and some attired as if they were attending a ball at the palace.

We paused outside a tent showing a drawing of a tiny person standing by a daffodil, and refreshed ourselves with a glass of juniper water. 'Shall we go to see this sideshow?' Anne asked. 'What does it say?'

I read from the printed notice: '*Inside sits a girl of sixteen years of age, not above eighteen inches long. She reads well, sings, whistles and all very pleasant to hear. You may see this wonderful creature for the sum of two pence.*'

'Oh, do let's go in!' Anne said.

I shook my head. 'It must be some trick,' I said, trying to peer around the curtain to see what was within. 'It cannot be a true person.'

'A girl as real as life!' the showman cried, seeing our interest. 'Only come in and see for yourself. And ladies only may see this creature in her shift.'

But Anne was now looking at the canvas booth next door, which was painted to look like a horse's stable and had, in fact, a real horse peering out of the flap on the door.

'What will happen here?' she asked me.

'*The Mare that counts money,*' I read out. '*Come and see this beast who is as clever as a man. She counts, gives wise advice on investments and imparts knowledge.*'

'That cannot be!' Anne said.

'No, it cannot,' I said, laughing.

'Come see the horse that counts!' the showman called. 'Wisdom truly from the horse's mouth!'

We walked on and Anne moved closer to me, for three chained lunatics came along, gibbering and dancing with a bear who wore irons on its legs. A man with them carried a notice which announced that they were released for the day from Bethlehem Hospital, which was a madhouse, and were available to come to the houses of the quality to amuse their guests for a small fee.

As we walked on my eyes were everywhere, darting through spaces and over people's heads, trying to see the one show that I was really looking for: was Count de'Ath going to be at the fair today?

A man passed with six or seven monkeys sitting all over him, and another wore the head of a great beast and carried a board which announced that all should repent of their sins, for this was the Year of the Beast and judgement was at hand.

Anne pointed towards a large tent with a board outside. 'B . . . best sh . . . show,' she began reading out haltingly, for I had been helping her with her letters and her reading and writing were slowly improving.

'. . . in the fair,' I continued. '*A wonderful curiosity. A man with one head and two bodies, both masculine, who is lately brought over from the country of the Moguls, and with him his brother who has hair down to his knees.*'

'I don't think I should care to see those,' Anne said. 'I would rather see the little creature as tall as a flower.'

'Or what about this,' I said, reading out from the next-door booth: '*A tableau recently come from Russia of curiously preserved people who are enchanted and lay between life and death. You may touch and examine these people as much as you wish for no extra charge.*'

Anne gasped. 'I should like to see those!'

There were more of the same at the other sideshows: dancing apes, a dog that played the tabor,

108

a man twice the size of a Lincolnshire heifer, a hare that did a morris dance, a woman with a prodigious beard. I could not see the Count and his magic cabinet, however.

After much deliberation we decided to go into the booth with the Russian tableau for, as Anne said, we would get several people for the price of one. Paying our money, we went behind a curtain and came across a strange scene, which so startled me that I turned to go out again, thinking that we had somehow gone the wrong way and strayed into some lady's drawing room by mistake.

In the tent was a long upholstered sofa, and on this sat three people: two women and a man. Each was exquisitely dressed in velvet and satins, and each engaged in drinking tea, either holding a cup to their lips or conveying it delicately towards its saucer.

This in itself was not strange. What was most surprising, though, was that none of the people was moving, but rather seemed frozen in that moment, each teacup neither touching their lips nor ever reaching its destined saucer. More strange still – for people could, mayhap, play at statues, but *animals* couldn't – there was a golden-haired lapdog sitting on one of the lady's laps, its pink tongue hanging forth and its head coyly on one side.

'Oh!' Anne breathed and, after standing in silence staring at them staring at us, we circled the trio, examining them minutely.

'They do not breathe,' Anne said timidly. 'Are they alive?'

'They do not even blink!' I said, passing my hand in front of the man's eyes.

Daringly, I put out a hand to touch the hand of the woman. It was smooth and cool, almost like skin but not quite.

'It *looks* like skin,' I said, peering at her cheek as closely as I dared, for I was in a mind to think that these people were enchanted and would be released from their spell in a moment and chastise us for examining them so rudely.

We tiptoed around them, looking at their hair, their clothes and their shoes. Every aspect of them was considered and refined. One of the ladies was wearing mules and I could see the tips of her toes, pink-painted, while the other carried a little silver-mesh bag in which could be seen her red lip-crayon and patch box.

'Is one of them the sleeping beauty who was put under a wicked spell?' Anne asked in awe.

I shook my head. 'I don't know,' I said wonderingly, 'but they are mighty strange.'

The entrance curtain was just then pulled aside again and two well-dressed ladies came into the show, starting with fright just as we had done at the sight of the trio there.

Then one began to laugh. 'Do not fear – they are made of wax!' she said to her companion. 'I have seen similar at Southwarke Fair.'

'But so real!' said her friend in awe.

'I believe the maker is a skilled artist who does likenesses on tombs.'

The other said, shuddering, 'I don't like them. They're too lifelike for me.'

'Too death-like!' corrected the first as they went out.

Anne and I now looked again, rather disappointed, at the wax statues. 'Then they're not enchanted sleeping beauties,' she said.

I shook my head. 'I suspect that little in this fair is what it seems to be.'

Feeling hungry, we went to Pie Corner and had hot pasties and a dish of peas, followed by gilt gingerbread and buttered ale, all of which were excellent. We saw a Dog Toby dance the hornpipe, then Jacob Hall – who was rumoured to be the lover of several high-born ladies – performing on a tight-rope high in the air and making everyone scream with fright at his antics. We heard bands and bagpipes, kettledrums and fiddlers, and saw many more sights, including the educated ape of whom Mr Newbery had spoken.

Anne then found a gypsy who, on her hand being crossed with a piece of silver, promised to tell you who you would marry and how many children you would have, and said she would return your money if it didn't come true.

'Oh do let me go!' Anne implored me. 'She says she sees spirits walk and fairies dance – and I do so want to know who I'll marry.'

'But it costs a piece of silver!' I said. 'And how will you get your money back from her if none of it comes true?'

Anne looked shocked. 'She is a high-born gypsy queen!' she said. 'She has second sight. Of course it'll come true.'

I might have relented and gone to the gypsy as well (for of course I, too, was anxious to know if I would marry) but then, at last, I saw on the edge of the field a board announcing *Count de'Ath and his Magick Cabinet.*

I steered Anne away from the gypsy. 'We will go later perhaps,' I said. 'But for now we must go and find the man I came to see.'

The Count was standing on some steps by his tent, which was of a large oval shape and looked as if it could contain a hundred people. Tall, dark and strange-looking, he was pointing with a stick at the words on the board before him. I read them out to Anne. *'An enchantment so strong that men can be turned to air! See someone enter my cabinet and be transported over land and sea, never to return!'*

'You're not going into that cabinet!' Anne said in sudden fright, putting her arm round my waist. 'I shan't let you go!'

'Of course I'm not going in it,' I said. 'I just want to see the magic performed again, and perhaps speak to the Count.'

The board announced a show starting on the stroke of every hour, and we paid our three pence and entered, ready to wait the twenty minutes or so. Evidently Count de'Ath had quite a following, for there was already a small crowd inside sitting on benches and waiting for three o'clock.

We sat towards the back and began talking of all the sights we had seen that day, and indeed were glad of the rest in the cool darkness of the tent, which was lined in some black cloth and had only some tapers to light it.

More people entered, and then it was three o'clock and Count de'Ath himself came through from outside and walked on to the small wooden stage at the front, where his cabinet stood ready. As before, he went through the same talk – asking if there was anyone who wanted to escape from his wife or creditors and saying they could enter his cabinet and be transported away.

As before, no one in the audience moved.

He asked again for someone to enter the box. 'And ze price vill merely be your soul,' he added.

There were a few gasps, then an eerie silence, as if everyone were holding their breath.

I scanned the front rows. No one. No one who looked like Tom.

But then someone got to his feet. 'I will go!' a man called. 'I will leave this land of horror and plague, and if I lose my soul then so be it!'

The man who'd spoken was a monk, in rough brown habit tied with rope and a deep hood over his head which half-concealed his face. A stir ran around the audience at seeing his garb. 'A holy monk to lose his soul!' Anne said, shocked, for indeed it did seem terrible that a man of God should have truck with the Devil's work.

Count de'Ath spent some moments telling the monk exactly when it would be necessary to extract payment for the journey he would be making, and how there was no going back on this strange bargain, and through it all I sat enraptured, listening to everything, watching avidly and hardly breathing, so intense was my scrutiny of everything that was happening on the stage. The man would go to Hell, sure as anything. How desperate he must be!

Two men from the audience examined the cabinet carefully, tapping it back and front, and then the monk silently turned and entered it. It was then that my heart stood still, for under the hood I saw that it was Tom, and no other.

How could this be?

Amazed and unbelieving, I wanted to call out, yet could not, for I felt as frozen and petrified as the wax people we had seen. The curtain was pulled across, concealing the monk from view. Count de'Ath muttered something in a strange language and then a moment passed, the curtain was opened again and the monk was gone.

Several women in the audience screamed and there was a groan from a man in front of us.

'Oh, where has he gone?' Anne whispered.

Count de'Ath bowed stiffly, then the audience was dismissed and began to shuffle out, looking mystified and amazed.

'Real enchantment!' Anne said wonderingly. 'Now that was proper magic, wasn't it?'

'I . . . I do not know.'

She stood up and tugged at my hand. 'Where shall we go now?'

I didn't move, for I was confused, and couldn't come to terms with all that was in my head. First Tom was dead, then I saw him go into a magic cabinet at the theatre and vanish, then he appeared as a monk – and then disappeared again.

Was he really dead?

Had he become a monk?

Had he sold his soul?

'Come on!' Anne said. 'We must see more things before it gets dark.'

I shook my head. 'I have something I must do. I

think . . . I think I know the person who went into the cabinet.'

'What?' Anne looked at me strangely. 'How do you know a monk?'

'He may not be a monk.' I shook my head as if to clear it. 'Wait for me, Anne. I have to go to see Count de'Ath.'

I ran outside, but the Count was not yet back on his stand at the front of the tent trying to entice people for the next performance, so I went around to the back. Here there was a square canvas tent about as tall as a man, with a flap-door tied up with rope. Someone was within, that was certain, for the canvas was moving about as if someone were divesting themselves of their clothing.

'Count de'Ath?' I enquired uncertainly, and then, 'Tom?'

The movement ceased.

'Tom?' I asked again, 'is it you?' And at once a surge of joy and certainty ran through me so that I felt filled with light and happiness. 'It's Hannah.'

The canvas door was pushed aside and Tom was there looking at me in disbelief: he was thin, pale and shorn of his hair, but not dead at all. Not a monk. Nor changed into air and transported over seas.

'Tom!' I said, a sob half-choking me. 'It's really you. I thought you were dead!'

'I thought *you* were!'

And then losing all modesty, I put my arms around his thin frame and held him as if I would never let him go.

From beside us, there was a drawn-out gasp. 'What's happening and who is this?' Anne's voice asked. Neither of us answered and a moment later her tone changed and became pert and lively. 'Oh, Hannah! Is this your sweetheart?'

Still holding on to him tightly, I managed to nod. 'Yes, Anne. Yes, this is Tom.'

Chapter Nine

2nd September

'My maid called us up about three in the morning to tell us of a great fire they saw in the City. So I rose and went to the window . . . but thought it far enough off and so went to bed again and to sleep.'

The following day I was in an agony of suspense as I waited for Tom to arrive – mostly because I could hardly believe that he was really coming. When I'd woken that morning it had seemed to me that I'd imagined the whole thing and had only dreamt that I'd found him at the fair, for to meet someone you thought was dead seemed a strange and incredible thing – and to discover that person in the cabinet of a magician even more fantastical. It was only Anne's questioning of me as soon as my eyes were open that told me that it had really happened.

'But what do you *think* he was doing there?' she asked, leaning up on one elbow in our bed to stare at me.

I shook my head, still as baffled as she.

'Is he really a monk? Did he not go into that

cabinet? How could he just disappear from it and be outside all the time?'

'I don't know, I don't know, I don't know!' I said.

'Will he really come round today?'

'He promised he would . . .'

Rising, I found we were out of water, so I threw a shawl over my nightshift and went down to the well at the end of the lane to draw some. As I walked back, I swung the buckets I carried and felt like bursting out singing. Tom was alive. I'd found him. He hadn't died of plague at all!

The afternoon before, when I'd stopped crying, he'd peeled my arms away gently and told me to go to the front of the stand before Count de'Ath came and found us speaking.

'I will explain all to you tomorrow,' he'd said. 'Are you living at the shop again?'

I'd nodded. 'But do you truly promise to come to me?'

'I truly promise! It's Sunday and the fair will be closed. The Count owes me some free time.'

'But how have you—'

'It's been a deal of do,' he'd said, 'but I will tell all tomorrow. Go now, or I'll lose my job!'

Now, as I carried the water into our shop, Mr Newbery was just coming out of his. He was not wearing his wig and his face was fuddled with sleep, his eyes rheumy.

I bade him good morning, but he scowled at me and held his head, and I guessed he had spent overlong at the alehouse the previous night. I was very anxious to tell someone my news, however. 'Anne and I enjoyed Bartholomew Fair, Mr Newbery!' I said. 'And the most surprising and excellent thing – you remember my friend Tom who worked with Doctor da Silva the apothecary along the lane?'

'The 'pothecary died of plague,' he said gruffly. 'And so did his lad.'

'But he *didn't*, though,' I said. 'For I found him at the fair. Tom, my sweetheart!'

He grunted. 'Is he much changed and crippled by having the sickness?'

'Hardly changed at all!'

'Then the disease went inside,' he said, nodding sagely. 'More than likely he will be mad.'

I could do naught but laugh. 'He's not mad at all! He's as sensible as you and I and he's coming round today!'

But Mr Newbery just gave another grunt and shuffled off down the road.

By the time the bell-man rang two o'clock, though, I was getting concerned. Anne and I had spent the morning busily preparing frosted petals and making several violet cakes with some flowers we'd bought at the fair, but by noon our rooms were straight and I was ready – more than ready, for indeed I'd changed my dress several times. Though I loved my green taffeta gown best of all, I remembered that Tom had seen this when we'd walked out the previous year, so felt compelled to change into my tabby suit. I then thought my blue linen gown might be more suitable (for it was another hot day) but once it was on me I found that it had several spots on it – from Anne wearing it – so changed back once again into my green taffeta.

All this was regarded very closely by Anne, who watched me with interest and then offered me patches and hair pomade, both of which I turned down. I put some orange flower water behind my ears and a little rose oil on my lips, however, and did not think this too immodest.

'Are you sure he'll come?' she asked, as I settled for the green, hung up my other gowns and swore I would not change again. 'For I still don't understand how he *can*, for he was supposed to be changed into air and sent over lands and seas . . .'

'I don't know either,' I said, walking once again to the shutters and peering out. 'But I believe he'll come.'

By the time the crier called three I was fair distracted out of my mind, but a little after this we heard a tap on the door. Anne sprang to it and flung it open before I could pose myself, for I had thought to be seated demurely with Kitty on my lap, but instead was seen crouched down engaged in picking something off my shoe.

Tom stood in the doorway and removed his hat and bowed, and I rose hastily and curtseyed, which actions seemed formal and strange to me, seeing as I had spent some moments the previous afternoon sobbing in his arms. But then he came over and kissed my cheek and took my hand in his, and we sat together on the wooden bench in the shop, with Anne on the chair a little distance off, surveying us with interest.

'I'm sorry to be later than I wanted to be,' he said. 'I had to run an errand on the way and got tangled in a crowd near the river, for there's much astir there.'

'Why's that?' Anne asked.

'I heard that there's a fire near to the wharves.'

'There are always fires there,' I said. 'There was one at the tallow-chandlers last week which gutted the place right out.'

'Is it a big fire?' Anne asked.

'I couldn't see it. But someone roused the Lord Mayor in the night to tell of it and ask for the fire-squirts to be brought, and he looked on it and said it was nothing and that a woman might piss it out.'

Anne and I laughed, but Tom suddenly looked embarrassed. 'You must pardon me for using such a term,' he said, 'but I have not had female company for many a month and I have almost forgot my manners.'

'Then you *are* a monk?' Anne asked.

'No, I am not.'

'Oh! And you didn't go into the cabinet and get turned into air?'

Smiling, he shook his head. 'No. But you mustn't tell a soul that it's not true.'

'*None* of it is true?' Anne and I both asked at once.

'None of it.'

'Not magic?' Anne said, disappointed.

'I will tell you all, and tell you truly,' he said. 'But first let me ask where is your sister Sarah, and what happened to you after you left London?'

I took a deep breath. 'It's a long story,' I said, and attempted to tell him in as few words as possible (for I was more than anxious to hear *his* tale) about our stay in Dorchester at the pesthouse, and then at Highclear, and our journey home when Sarah had met Giles Copperly, and then about me and Anne coming to London. 'And when I reached London I was told that both you and Doctor da Silva had contracted plague

121

and were dead!' I finished.

Tom was silent a while. 'Doctor da Silva died, God rest his soul,' he said then. 'I was thought to be dead, too – and even taken for a ride on a death cart.'

'You were put on the death cart?' I gasped, while Anne sat open-mouthed.

He nodded. 'The Doctor had already died and I was unconscious when they took up our bodies with some others to convey us to the pit,' he said. 'Luckily for me, though, the buboes under my arm had burst and the poison was slowly draining from me, so that when the cart reached the pit I had recovered my wits enough to sit up and ask for a pigeon pastie.'

I tried to laugh with him yet could not, for his dying was not a matter in which I could find humour.

'I lay abed for some weeks until I was strong enough to stir myself, and then I had to find a job. I heard at a hiring fair that Count de'Ath wanted a thin, strong lad, so applied for the position.' He stretched out his arms. 'Do you find me changed?'

I nodded. 'You are much thinner, yes, and taller – and you have no hair to speak of.'

'That is because I lost my hair to the plague and it is only just now growing again. But I have reason to thank the sickness for my present job, for only a very thin person could fit into the secret space at the back of the cabinet, and on that my job depends.'

'So you just go into the back of the cabinet?' Anne said, looking affronted. 'There is no magic to it at all?'

He shook his head. 'I'm afraid not.'

She sighed heavily. 'It is too bad to think there's no magic in the world.'

'There *is* magic.' Tom's eyes caught mine and locked

122

with them. 'For those who are lucky. But it is not a matter of cabinets and disappearing monks.'

Tom and I went for a walk. I longed to go to Chelsea again, where we had spent a day last year picking wild flowers, but the sun was already low in the sky and the walk would have taken several hours. Instead we went out of the City by Ludgate and took a route past the prison and over Fleet River (which was stinking very bad after the hot summer we had had) and from there to the Strand to admire the new-built houses of the nobility. We came near to the king's palace at Whitehall and I told Tom about coming back to London on May Day, and seeing His Majesty on the royal barge.

'May Day.' Tom frowned slightly, trying to remember. 'I was in Bath then, appearing at the pleasure gardens.'

'With Count de'Ath?' I asked.

He nodded. 'I've been with him for six months now.'

'Is he a good man?'

Tom raised his eyebrows. 'A cat will be a cat still,' he said.

I looked at him for his meaning.

'He is as good as any quack can be, but he is not a real Count, and not even French.' He smiled. 'When he is not Count de'Ath he is Doctor Marvell. Have you heard of Doctor Marvell's excellent medicine?'

'No!' I said, laughing.

'Doctor Marvell's medicine can cure everything from rupture to measles and from toothache to the bladder stone,' Tom said solemnly. 'Three bottles will fit a man for life and cure any illness he is likely to encounter during all of that time.'

'Can it cure plague?' I asked.

'Everything!' he said firmly, with the glint of a smile in his eye.

'And what is in this wonderful linctus?'

'Nettle water.'

'What's that?'

'A few leaves of nettle steeped in water. And perhaps a leaf of curled parsley for luck.'

I began to laugh. 'That will not cure anyone!'

'But 't'will not kill anyone, either. And if you think it is doing you good then mayhap it will. It'll do the quack doctors good, certainly,' he went on, 'for there were a hundred different cures for plague and men were made rich by them.'

'But why did you not take up a new apprenticeship with another apothecary?' I asked after a moment.

'Because there was no one to pay my premium,' he said. 'When I recovered from plague I journeyed home, but could not find my father and stepmother. I was told they had moved away.' His voice broke slightly and I squeezed his hand and looked at him with tenderness, for I could see that he had felt himself alone in the world. 'But I get on well with Count de'Ath,' he said with more cheer, 'and it is a merry job, for when I am not making bottles of nettle water then I am an actor.'

'So it's always you who appears and goes into the cabinet?'

He nodded. 'Sometimes I'm a monk, sometimes I'm a farmer, on occasion I'm a woman! I have six changes of face and keep a record of what person I am

124

where, for I must never appear in the same guise twice in the same place.'

'I saw you at the theatre dressed as a dandy,' I said. 'At least, it seemed to be someone who looked much like you. That was partly why we came to Bartholomew Fair – so I could see the show again.'

He smiled. 'I'm very glad that you did.'

I hesitated a moment. 'What I cannot understand,' I said slowly, 'is that seeing how you were alive all the time, you did not come round to the shop to see me.'

'I did!' he said. 'I came when we were in London earlier this year – in February or March.'

'Oh! We were still in Dorset then . . .'

'I came round in a rush, dressed as a monk, and spoke to your neighbour – the frowsy-headed fellow at the sign of the Parchment and Quill.'

'Mr Newbery.'

'And he told me you were dead for sure, and he might take over your shop if no one claimed it.'

'The hog-grubber!' I gasped. And then I looked at Tom from under my eyelashes. 'But did you just come round to ask for me once only?' I asked, for this did not seem to me to be enough.

He smiled, his head on one side. 'And did you enquire after *me* once only?' he countered.

'Indeed not!' I said indignantly. 'I saw that Doctor da Silva's shop was shuttered, and spoke to an old lady who said that you'd gone to the pesthouse and died, and then I enquired at the pesthouse and saw it recorded that the death cart had taken you!' I paused. 'But how many times did you ask for me?'

'I was at Death's door for six weeks – so you will excuse me not asking *then*,' he said, laughing a little, 'and then I was travelling across England, to Bath and Warminster and Canterbury to all the fairs and theatres that Count de'Ath could reach. I came to enquire about you both times we were in London, however – the first when I spoke to your neighbour and once again, late one afternoon after we'd appeared at the King's Theatre. I banged at your door but although it was a trading day the shop was still shut and boarded, so I feared that you must really be dead.'

'It was shut and boarded because I was at the theatre seeing you!' I said. 'Nelly Gwyn had been in the shop and given us tickets for that very day.'

We mock-glared at each other, then this gave way to laughter and thence – in myself at least – to something close to tears, for we had so nearly lost each other, and it had been only the most peculiar set of circumstances which had caused us to find each other again.

I wiped my eyes with my fingers and Tom pulled a linen kerchief out of his pocket for me, and with it came a length of bright green silk ribbon.

'For me?' I gasped. 'How pretty!'

'No, it is for my new disguise . . .' Tom began, and then he stopped and lifted my chin, for my face had fallen in disappointment. 'No, indeed it is not! I was only teasing, for I bought it yesterday at the fair. And there is a silver locket too, which is to go on the ribbon and be tied around your neck.'

'Oh!' I said, and could not say more or even thank him because I was quite speechless with pleasure and happiness.

'And I'm glad you're wearing this green gown, for I bought it specially to match it,' he added.

We had walked a good way out of the City by this time, and were in a pretty lane alongside the Thames where Michaelmas daisies grew amass in blue, purple and white clumps. There was a fallen oak tree covered in all manner of ferns and ivies, and we sat upon this and Tom carefully threaded the locket on to the ribbon and tied it around my neck. When it was tied fast his hands moved from around my neck to my face, one finger tracing along the line of my cheek, another trembling on my lips. I lifted my face to his, seeing the sun shimmering the sky crimson and dappling the river with light, and then, as I closed my eyes, his mouth came down softly upon mine.

My first kiss was everything I'd dreamed it would be, and there were two more kisses after it before Tom took a deep breath and said that we ought to be getting back.

'That's what I was thinking,' I said quickly, although I hadn't at all, but did not want him to think of me as a girl ready to throw up her petticoats at any man's asking.

'We'll be together again soon,' he said.

I felt the locket at my neck and ran my fingers over its cool smooth shape, impatient to get home and look at it properly, for I had not had time to see it before he'd put it on me. 'Will we?' I asked. 'For you'll be travelling around all the time with Count de'Ath.'

'Well, we are at Bartholomew Fair all this week, and then go over the river to Southwarke, and from there to Richmond – and I can come and see you from all those places.'

'But what then?' I asked, for I felt I couldn't let him go.

'Then . . .' He shrugged. 'I don't know. With the winter coming mayhap the Count will shore up somewhere for a season. And London is where the money is to be made, so we may stay here.'

I sighed. 'But what if it—'

He interrupted me by kissing me again, lightly, on my nose. 'Wait and see. If I go away then I'll give you a kiss for each freckle and this will last us until we meet again.'

And with this I had to be content.

Walking downriver a little, we came to a landing stage where several boatmen were plying their trades ferrying people across to the other bank, and Tom negotiated a fare of sixpence with a young water-dog for us to be taken as far as Swan Steps at London Bridge. It started off a pleasant trip, for although the sun had almost disappeared, it was still warm with a light breeze, and a soft mist was rising from each bank of the river. There were craft aplenty: families out with their servants, couples deep in each other's eyes, and groups of young men carousing.

It was only when we were coming to the last deep bend of the Thames before the City that we became aware that all was not as it should be. The craft we were seeing were not bent on pleasure; some were being rowed hard, with a purpose, across to the other bank or upstream and away. And then as we came around the river's bend we heard strange sounds: the clashing noise of church bells reverse-pealing, and an awkward crackling sound tempered by the occasional sharp bang of what sounded like fireworks.

Our water-dog hailed another to ask what was amiss, saying that he had only just now begun his evening's work.

'Fire!' the other yelled back. 'Some of the wharves are alight and you'll not be able to land at Swan Steps.'

Our water-dog swore, and said he would land us wherever he could and the rest of the trip could go hang, and so began to row us towards the bank.

As we cleared the bend we could see the fire for ourselves, as it was sending up pillars of smoke in a line all along the river from Black Swan Alley, where I sometimes went for sugar, past Cold Harbour as far as London Bridge. In all, the flames looked to stretch for a quarter of a mile or more.

'This must be the fire that I told you of this morning!' Tom said as we both stared in horror at the bank. 'I had no idea it was this bad.'

''Tis more fire than I have ever seen at once!' I gasped.

The boatman began to swear under his breath for, although he was rowing as fast and as hard as he could, backwards and forwards, he could not find a landing stage which was not crowded with people intent on putting out to river and getting away.

'Your fare will be double!' he shouted to Tom, and Tom could not but agree to pay him.

Up and down the river we rowed without finding a place to alight, and once the boatman threatened to put us out on the Southwarke side of the river, and upped his fare to one shilling and sixpence not to do so. Tom again agreed to pay, for the north side of the bridge was now burning hard, its glistening timbers falling, splashing and sizzling into the water, and we knew we would not get across it if we were landed on the Southwarke side.

Once we were close by to the river banks we could see people running along Fish Hill and Thames Street, some of them pushing their furniture on carts, or carrying chairs atop of their heads. Two or three churches were alight, too, their steeples standing black like witches' hats with the flames rushing up them, and even old Dyers Hall was afire with orange and gold flames reaching towards the sky. As I looked in wonderment and fear at this mighty building, the roof fell in with a terrible crash and a great cloud of dust and golden sparks lifted into the sky. A gust of wind wafted these across to a row of houses in Black Raven Alley, and I saw some thatched roofs catch and then a man running along the street with his clothes alight.

I clasped Tom's arm tightly, for I was much afraid, and it looked for a while as if we would not be able to land at all. In a few moments, however, the boatman put us out a little downriver at Broken Wharf Steps, his boat being immediately taken by two men who were intent on getting away and did not care where. I heard the boatman demand from them the sum of five shillings, and I did not doubt that he would get it, for the men seemed in a passion of fear.

As we reached the top of the steps I looked back to the river. Dense smoke was now hanging over the water like a fog, and sparks and fragments of burning wood and cloth were falling into it, hissing and spluttering. The rising moon showed a family standing by the waterside throwing all their possessions into a wherry: table, chairs, clothes, bedding – all went in. The moon then gleamed crimson and a moment later vanished under billowing clouds of smoke, and the family disappeared into the dark so that I did not see what happened to them.

Tom and I stood speechless, hardly knowing where to go or what to do.

In the streets running alongside the river, all was chaos and noise and stink – for the glue-makers were by this wharf and there was an acrid smell of burning bones and animal fat here. Fires roared to the right of us, windows shattered, barrels exploded and stones of buildings fragmented and fell. The street was thronged with people bent double under the weight of the goods they bore on their backs, or pushing hand carts with furniture atop. I saw a sick man lying on a pallet, moaning as he was carried along, and a whole family of ten or so children sitting on a farm cart, crying with fear.

An old woman was standing outside the door of her house looking around her in wonder, and Tom stopped to speak to her.

'What's happening here now?' he asked. 'Is anyone fighting the fire?'

'Oh, 'tis all in fair order,' she nodded, 'for the king is now come to fight it with his brother the Duke. They have ordered the pulling down of all houses in its path.' She cocked her head to one side. 'If you listen you can hear the crashes.'

'But where did the fire start?'

'Over east a way – Pudding Lane. In a baker's shop, so I've heard.'

'But you must leave here!' I said to her. 'The wind's blowing the fire in this direction.'

'I'll go just as soon as I've seen the king and spoken to him,' said the old woman.

'But he may not have time to speak to everyone! You must shift for yourself and go now!'

'There's plenty of time,' she said comfortably. 'Yon fire is more than two streets away.'

It seemed useless to argue with her, and Tom pulled at my hand. 'Come, Hannah,' he said. 'We must get back and see what danger there is for your shop. And for Anne.'

We were nigh exhausted by the time we reached the shop, for the streets near the river had been teeming with people, carts and horses trying to get away, and we'd sometimes had to employ our hands and elbows to fight our way through. Strangely, though, as we left the river behind, the smoke and roaring and smell all receded, as did the reverse-pealing bells, so that by the time we reached Crown and King Place and I saw our dear shop sign, all was calm and quiet, with no indication anywhere that there was a fire raging elsewhere in the City.

I hammered on the door. 'Are you all right?' I asked Anne, as she opened the door. 'Is all well here?'

'Of course,' she said, and I saw her eyes fall on the silver locket and widen. 'Why?'

'The fire!'

'What fire?' she asked.

Tom laughed. 'See. All's well. It will likely be put out tonight and tomorrow they will start rebuilding. 'Tis always the way.'

He took my hand and kissed it. I'd rather he had kissed me on the lips but as Anne was watching us, had to be content. 'But when will I see you?' I asked.

'I'll come tomorrow. In the evening when the fair

closes,' he said, and he blew me another kiss and ran off.

I watched him go. 'He stays on the fair site at Smithfield,' I said to Anne, a trifle anxiously. ''Tis a way outside the City walls, so he should be safe.'

'Why shouldn't he be?'

'Don't you listen? Because of the fire raging!'

'But you heard what he said . . .' Her eyes fell upon the locket again and sparked with interest. 'Now let me look at that silver heart, and tell me straight what he said as he gave it to you and if he declared love, for I cannot wait a moment longer to know.'

Chapter Ten

The Fire Takes Hold

'Met my Lord Mayor in Canning Street, and he cried like a fainting woman, "Lord what can I do? I am spent! People will not obey me. I have been pulling down houses but the fire overtakes us faster than we can work."'

No crier came to wake us the next morning, but I was awake at first light anyway, wondering if the fire was still burning and if it was, where it was heading. We were at the western corner of the City and a goodly way from the last point I had seen flames, but anything could have happened by now. Tom, however, had seemed sure that it would have been put out overnight, and I prayed that this would be so.

Tom. I felt for the locket around my neck, held it tightly between my fingers and wished on it that he would come to no harm. This thought of him led me to musing on his kisses, and I was about to begin going over them precisely, moment by moment, when there was a knock – nay, a hammering – on the shop door. Leaving Anne still dozing, I slid out of bed, pulled a shawl around myself and went to open it.

Mr Newbery stood there, fully dressed in his Sunday clothes of ribbon-edged breeches, doublet and cloak, with plumed hat over his periwig.

'Fire!' he pronounced gravely. 'A very desperate fire.'

I nodded. 'I saw it last night by the river.'

'And spreading north and like to engulf us all!'

'It will surely not spread as far as us,' I said. 'For isn't the king himself working to fight it now?'

'The king!' Mr Newbery said scornfully. 'This fire is a condemnation of that very man. It has been long said that this year has the number of the Beast and will contain a judgement against him and his depraved court!'

I didn't say anything to this but put on my listening face, for I knew a discourse was coming.

'The court did not change their ways so the Lord brought down a plague and a pestilence. And now he brings a fire to cleanse their souls.' He paused and added in a more general tone, 'What's more, the king has now acknowledged another royal bastard. That makes six of 'em that we know about!'

I stepped out on to the cobbles to look into the sky, which was white and milky with smoke and contained a pale and ineffective sun. There was a strong stench of burning in the air and, as I stood there, a flurry of paper, charred at the edges, dropped out of the sky around us.

'So it burns still!' I said.

'That is just what I've been saying,' he retorted. 'And I must rouse all our neighbours that haven't yet heard of it.'

Two lads passed us in a great hurry, and Mr Newbery hailed them and asked where they went.

'To Whitehall,' one of them called. 'The people are making a deputation for His Majesty to use greater measures to save them from the fire.'

'What can *he* do?' Mr Newbery asked scornfully. 'He is only one man.'

'He is the anointed king!' they said, as if this were enough in itself to preserve us all.

'And 'tis his fault we're stricken in the first place,' Mr Newbery muttered as they went on.

Anne had now stirred herself and came to stand beside me in the doorway. 'Oh! How big is the fire now?' she asked, looking up at the sky. 'Do we still open the shop this morning?'

I shrugged, looking at Mr Newbery for advice. 'I don't know.'

'People still have to eat,' he said. 'But I doubt if they will be eating sweetmeats. I myself intend to go to the market to buy some good cheese and some pies, in case the food markets are all closed tomorrow. And then I will pack the rest of my clothes and my possessions lest I have to flee.'

'Then we must do the same,' I said to Anne.

Mr Newbery licked his finger and held it high for a moment. 'The wind is changing,' he announced. 'It now blows towards the west of the City.'

'Where is the west?' Anne asked.

'Where we are, my good child!'

'But it's a way off yet, isn't it?' I said. 'It may yet be halted – or the wind may change again.'

'Or it may not,' Mr Newbery said.

I looked at him helplessly. 'Is there nothing more

that people can do to help themselves?' I asked.

He shrugged. 'If we had fire squirts we could dowse our houses – but there are none to be had.'

'What else?'

'The booksellers and stationers around St Paul's have taken their stocks and put them into the crypt,' he went on, 'and people are burying their treasured possessions in their gardens so that if the fire comes it will pass over them – indeed I passed a man burying his Parmesan cheese in his garden only yesterday. I myself am taking some of my best things to St Dominic's, so that they may lay safe within its walls.'

'But I saw churches on fire . . .' I said, speaking slowly, for it had just occurred to me that if this fire was a judgement from God, why was He also burning His own churches?

Mr Newbery shrugged. 'Goods will be safer there, stacked tight, than in our flimsy shops,' he said, and then went on his way to warn and befright our other neighbours. And indeed perhaps this was a good thing.

Anne and I got dressed quickly, hardly bothering to wash ourselves, for such was the smoke and smut in the air that to do so seemed a waste of time. I put on my old grey linen dress, which I cared for least, and carefully folded the others in case I should need to flee with them. I then made Anne do the same. After this we took a box and put in it the few things we valued: our kitchen equipment, chafing dishes, pans and bowls. We also took our canvas travelling bags, putting in them those hair combs, fans, favourite gloves, perfumes and odds and ends that are precious to those of the female sex.

Going out for provisions (for I could already see that there were very few bakers or milkmaids around), I decided we should head for Green Place, which was north of the City and just within the walls, rather than go towards the river where the fire seemed to be worst.

Although only one hour or so had passed since my conversation at the door with Mr Newbery, already the air outside was thicker. People seemed unsure of what they should do or where they should go, and several of our neighbours were standing around in little groups talking, glancing often down towards the City, where sometimes could be heard the dead-pealing of bells or a thudding gunpowder-bang where a house had been blown up to try and create a fire break.

We'd not taken more than a few steps when I suddenly remembered Kitty, who'd been curled asleep in a drawer.

'Shall we take her out with us in the basket?' Anne asked eagerly.

I shook my head. 'But we must go and close our back door and keep her inside,' I said. 'We can't risk her straying.'

Anne went back in to make her safe and at that moment a gang of men came running along the lane, some ten or twelve of them, carrying staves and sticks.

'The Frenchman!' I heard one shout. 'Where is he?'

I made to slip back inside our door, for I could see they meant business, but one of them saw me.

'The Frenchman – where does he live?' a heavy-set man shouted at me.

'I don't know of any Frenchman living down here,'

I said, shrinking back.

'There are no foreigners about!' Mr Gilbert, one of our neighbours, called over.

'Yes there is! Maurice is his name,' said the heavy-set man.

I shook my head again and tried to go inside again, but he took my arm. 'If you see him, tell him he'll hang for this.'

'We'll hang him ourselves!' another cried. 'And draw and quarter him as well.'

'What has he done?' Mr Gilbert asked.

'Fired our city. Put an incendiary through a window and set London alight!'

There was an angry murmur from our neighbours at this. 'There's a lodging house at the corner. Over the milliner's shop,' one said. 'He may be there.'

As the men ran off Mr Gilbert called to me that it wasn't safe to be a foreigner in London now, for gangs were seeking out any French and Dutch and accusing them of starting the fire. 'They even seized on an Italian washerwoman and threw her into the river!' he added.

Anne and I made our purchases without difficulty, for Green Place was where the country housewives came to sell their garden produce and their baking, and there were many more there that day who had not been willing to venture further into the City.

We stayed some time gossiping, for some folk there had already been made homeless by the fire and had tales to tell, and there were also those whose houses and shops were now in direct line with the fire and so were on their way out of the City. As in the plague, I saw that it was the poor who suffered most, for they had no carriages or carts to convey their goods or themselves away, nor place to go, and so these newly homeless were making their way to Moore Fields or London Fields to lie until the fire was brought under control.

We gathered around one woman who was telling of how she had seen the king himself amid the flames. 'He was stripped to his linen undershirt!' she said, 'passing buckets of water from the river to try and dowse the fire at Apothecaries Hall. His brother the Duke was alongside him, and both looking the very essence of masculinity and strength.'

'How did you know it was the king?' one asked. 'Was he wearing his crown?'

'Or was there an actress alongside o' him to rub salve into his burns?'

There was laughter before the woman replied with dignity that she knew it was he because a fine black horse had been standing alongside, held by a groom, and the horse's saddle and blanket had borne the royal standard.

Another housewife told of the looting which was going on in the Halls of the Guilds. 'At Dyers Hall, as soon as the fire had cooled, looters came crunching across the ashes and took away all the melted gold and silver they could handle.'

'I heard this too!' another joined in. 'And some twelve full suits of armour have been seen going downriver on a barge.'

'I saw a man killed over the hire of a cart!' one volunteered. 'Two men were bidding the owner five shillings . . . ten shillings . . . then the sum was one pound, and it went up and up until they had reached ten pounds!'

There were murmurs of wonder at this.

'The owner gave the cart over to one of the men and took the money,' the tale-teller went on, 'whereupon the other took out a knife, stabbed him and ran off with the cart!'

'But there is plenty of money to be earned for honest labour!' a man on a stall sought to tell everyone. 'They've set up fireposts down in the City. Each is provisioned with beer and bread, and the king will give a shilling a day to each diligent man who helps fight the fire.'

'That's only because he's fair frighted out of his wits that it'll reach his palace,' one answered dourly.

'It'll not reach that far,' said the stall-holder, 'for they're now pulling down rows of houses in the fire's path with grappling irons.'

'But the flames have a mind of their own and leap over the gaps that are left!' a woman said. 'I've seen it with my own eyes leave two rows of houses untouched and start ablazing in a complete new spot.'

'I heard of a family who lost their direction in the darkness,' another offered. 'A heap of coal on the quay caught fire, sending thick rolling smoke everywhere, and yon folk ended up with their cart in a blind alley and were set upon by a marauding gang. All their furniture and possessions were taken from them!'

Anne and I listened to these tales with bated breath, scarce knowing if we should believe them or if the reports were exaggerated. Anne thought they could not all be true but I, having seen London in the grips of plague and encountered many and worse horrors, was inclined to believe them all.

Having completed our purchases, we both felt full of a strange restlessness and did not want to go back to the shop, for we did not feel we could follow our normal routine and begin frosting sweetmeats on a day such as this. Instead we decided to walk to the north of the City and see if we could climb the City walls and glimpse the fire from there, and thus find out whether it progressed or no, and if so, whether it approached us.

Smoke now hung directly over us like a cloud, and there was the distant rumble of thunder in the air. As we walked, every moment it seemed to grow hotter, and as the sun rose higher, it lost its pale face and became a strange and horrid red disk.

Anne glanced up at it. 'I don't like that sun,' she said with a shiver. 'It doesn't seem natural. Today seems like the day of judgement: the end of the world that the clergy sometimes speak on in church.'

I tried to reassure her but could not do so with any conviction, for the same thought had already occurred to me. I tried to remember what I'd read in the almanac in Highclear House about 1666 being the Year of the Beast, when a cleansing fire would be brought down. I also thought about what I'd said to Mother about London being as safe as houses . . .

When we reached the walls, we found that at any point along them, especially near a gate, the roadways were crowded with carts, carriages, sedan chairs, horses and people on foot, all carrying furniture and fighting and jostling with each other to get out, and thus we could not make much progress. The situation was not helped by a large number of people fighting to get *in*: those looking for their families, going to rescue things from their homes, and also porters, labourers, carters – anyone with a conveyance on wheels for, as we had been told, there was a deal of money to be made from the moving of furniture and possessions. At Cripplegate we found confusion and accidents and fighting crowds, and these at Moorgate and Bishopsgate too, and finally (after we had seen one family's horse fall and break its legs on a pile of abandoned furniture, also a poor cat running for its life with all its fur afire) decided to go to All Hallows church and climb the tower there.

Although on occasion clouded by gusts of smoke, we now had a view which was quite terrible in its aspect, for it could be seen that the whole northern shore of the Thames was aflame from beyond the bridge on our left as far as the sturdy bulk of Baynards Castle on our right. Seeing this dreadful sight, my eyes straightaway filled with tears, for it was most shocking and awful to see those wharves, lanes and alleys and those houses and rooms ablaze, or reduced to sticks and ashes, and to think what devastation and terror must be in the hearts of those who lived and worked there.

Anne and I held each other tightly, both quite speechless with shock. Now that I had witnessed this scene for myself, words could not convey how awful I found it, for it did truly seem as Anne had said: that the end of the world was nigh.

Once I had dragged my glance back from the shoreline of the Thames I realised that our view was unobscured only because there were now very few large buildings between us and the river. Churches were burnt away or still in flames, many Halls of the Guilds were razed, as were the noble buildings in Cornhill and even – I uttered a cry – the magnificent Royal Exchange had surrendered, for I knew well where it had been and it was there no more! Straightaway, the thought of the visit I'd paid there with Abby came to me: the vast marble edifice of stately columns and noble statues, the gaily dressed gallants and so-fine ladies gossiping in the courtyards, the immaculate little shops containing delicate and rare items – all gone!

But even that knowledge was diminished by Anne suddenly screaming and burying her face in my shoulder, pointing with a shaking arm towards the heart of the fire, where now could be seen a wall of flame, some fifty feet high, moving as swiftly as the wind and travelling east to west along a row of houses. As I watched, horror-struck, each building in its path caught and erupted one after the other, small volcanoes sending blizzards of sparks everywhere. Stone buildings were slower to catch, others – according to what was stored within – burned fast and mad. This running fire was only halted when it reached the grey mass that was Bridewell prison on the banks of the Fleet and, beating against this, could go no further.

Thus thwarted, the fire, like a terrible living beast, turned and began to move slowly northward in a maelstrom of heat and noise. Reaching what must have been a storehouse containing spices and peppers, there was a sudden soft explosion and then a shimmer of blue, purple and green in the air which was terrible in its beauty and strangeness and made me and Anne both cry out in wonder. A moment later, an amazing spicy scent filled the air which for a moment dominated the stench of sulphur and gunpowder.

All in all, we stood there some two hours, until the front line of the fire was a mile across and the banks of the Thames were clothed in fire almost as far as we could see. We stood overlong for, although the sight before us was terrible indeed, it was also compelling in its very terribleness. It had something of the air of a public execution about it: spectacle and drama mixed equally with horror and fear.

We might have stayed longer, but I was anxious to see how things stood back at the shop. When the wind changed direction slightly and began to blow thick, sulphurous smoke in our direction, making us cough, we decided to descend. As we did so, two pigeons with their wings still burning thudded down beside us.

'They stayed too long on their perches and caught alight,' a man remarked, and he picked them up by their singed feet and declared he would take them home for his dinner.

Chapter Eleven

The Raging Beast

'At four o'clock in the morning, my Lady Batten sent me a cart to carry away all my money and plate and best things . . . which I did, riding myself in my nightgown in the cart; and Lord, to see how the streets and the highways are crowded with people, running and riding and getting of carts to fetch away things . . .'

Anne, beside me on the wooden pew, moved and whimpered softly in her sleep. It was hot in the small church and crowded besides, and I had not been able to sleep at all for wondering what was going to happen to us.

Last night the wind had been blowing strongly in our direction, and there had been great discussion with our neighbours in Crown and King Place as to whether the fire, still some distance off, would reach us. Mr Newbery said it would, and declared he was off to Moore Fields to lie under a bush and be safe, but others said they were sure the fire would be stopped long before it came to us, and besides, there was a vast firebreak being constructed along Lombard Street and it would not get further than this.

Most of the neighbours wavered, swayed first by one argument, then by the other, then one old woman declared that the flames could burn her up if they cared to, for she had not moved for plague and would not move for fire either. In the end, though, only a few stayed on in their homes, while most went to take shelter in St Dominic's church, feeling that there was safety in numbers and we would be able to alert each other quickly in case of danger. Here we had ranged ourselves and our precious possessions (Kitty being amongst these) along the hard benches and tried to make ourselves comfortable. We shared our food companionably, sung some of the old songs to try to cheer us, and several men had firewatched through the night.

I had not heard from Tom the previous evening, but took some comfort from a neighbour telling me that because of the fire, Bartholomew Fair had not opened since Saturday and that most of the fairground folk had already moved off to a fresh site. I felt in my heart that the love we shared (for though unspoken, I felt it was that) meant that we would meet again – for surely we had not lost and then found each other for no good reason?

As I shifted in the pew and rubbed at my stiff neck, there came a scritching and a scratching from Kitty's basket at my feet. It was very dark, however, there being no candles lit, and I did not dare loosen the tied lid, for if I did so she would run off and hide herself in some chink in the church and we would never see her again.

I think I dropped off to sleep shortly before dawn, but when I awoke to the sound of someone calling eight o'clock, it was still dark because of the heavy smoke which surrounded us. For a moment I could not remember where I was, and then I jumped up with a start to find Anne awake and feeding Kitty a cup of milk. Fresh bread had also been delivered, for the king had decreed that every working baker was to bake for the masses who were without a hearth or home.

As we ate, news began coming in from passers-by about fighting and looting in the shops, and about where the flames had reached, and what had caught fire and what had been saved. The previous day Anne and I had seen the fire reach Bridewell Prison, and though its walls were still proving too sturdy to collapse, they were blazing from end to end. Here – alas – the fire had jumped over the high City walls and was now racing west down Fleet Street, devouring the fine merchants' houses that Tom and I had seen on the previous Sunday.

The wind still encouraged the fire towards the north and west of the City; it had not moved east more than two streets away from Pudding Lane where it had started (whether from a baker's failing to put out his oven properly or from a foreigner's incendiary we did not know). The only good news we had received was that London Bridge had so far been saved, for the fire had not burned more than four struts along before it reached a gap in the houses and been halted. There was fire all along the banks and wharves here, though, and strong danger of the Tower of London catching.

'The king's beasts in the menagerie roar to wake the Devil!' a young man with a sooted face and singed hair told us breathlessly. 'For no one dares go near them – and there is no place to move them!'

'Can't they be given some linctus or herbs to send them to sleep?' someone asked.

The young man shook his head. 'The fire rages all around and it is monstrous hot in their quarters – no one can bear the heat enough to get close to them. The beasts pace to and fro and oft-times throw themselves against the bars of their cages in their distress.'

'But suppose the fire breaks down their cages and they escape?' a woman asked him in some nervousness. 'There would be great apes and tigers running in the streets!'

The young man shook his head. 'They would be burned to death before that,' he said. 'And even now they may be dead from the smoke.'

'Then I wish the poor beasts a quick and painless end,' the woman said, 'for all dumb animals must be near out of their minds with terror.'

Hearing this, Anne and I picked up Kitty and put her straight back in her basket. We had lost our cat Mew to the plague, and I did not wish to lose Kitty to the fire.

As our neighbours gradually went from the church – either to go home or to make for safe ground – we fell to talking about what to do next. We had not cleared everything from the shop, and wondered if we should try to obtain a cart to collect our bed and our few pieces of furniture and bring them into the church for safety. On looking outside, however, it became obvious that we would never obtain any sort of conveyance, for everything with wheels had already been pressed into duty and was crowding the lanes around us in great muddle and confusion.

'Do you think that Mother knows about the fire?' Anne asked.

'She's sure to,' I said. 'They say that the smoke from London can be seen rising fifty miles away.'

'They'll be worried . . .'

I nodded, but we had no possible hope of getting word to them that we were safe, for we knew that the post office had been consumed by fire in the night.

I was alerted by some disturbance outside. 'Listen!' I took Anne's hand. 'What can you hear?'

She shrugged.

'The fire!' I said. 'I'll swear that's what it is.'

She put her head on one side and closed her eyes. 'Yes!' she said. 'It's roaring away like Father's furnace – and there are noises like walls crashing.'

I swallowed hard. 'And timber cracking and people screaming.' I began to pick up our things. 'It's coming on apace and we must go,' I said, trying to sound calm, even though my heart was beating mightily. 'There may be a last-minute dash to get out of the City and we must get to the gates.'

'What about the other things left in the shop?' Anne asked. 'What of our bed?'

'Never mind!'

A sudden shouting came from outside and a man, sweating heavily, his face burned and blistered, ran into the church.

'Cheapside has fallen to the fire!' he shouted to those few of us still there. ''Tis fallen!'

There was a general wail of despair at this and Anne looked at me questioningly. ''Tis the road which

150

comes into the city from Newgate,' I said to her. 'The great highway where the kings make their progress and where all the rich goldsmiths' and silversmiths' shops are.'

'But did they not try to save it?' someone asked the man.

'Damn you for a fat gutted dog!' he exploded. 'We've been working all night making a break, but the south side caught fire and all the houses collapsed together sending firebrands across the gap so that the north caught as well!' His voice broke into something like a sob. 'The painted signs collapsed, the windows shattered, the stones cracked and then the great timbered roofs fell and lit up the sky. London's greatest street has been razed to the ground and will never be again!'

We waited no longer after this, but took up our boxes, baskets and bundles and left the church in some haste. Outside hung a thick blanket of smoke and, the lanes being full of abandoned furniture and bundles, it was difficult to walk without falling over something. Every moment we would be jostled by those bearing furniture on their backs or pushed out of the way to allow a cart through. As we dodged through showers of falling sparks, we found it difficult to breathe, for each full breath in made us cough or choke.

At first we just followed where the crowds were going, but then I stopped to think which might be the best gate to head for. We knew the fire had jumped the walls near Ludgate, and was now heading down Cornhill towards Newgate, so it seemed best to me to head towards Moorgate and thence to the safety of

Moore Fields. Accordingly, we turned at the corner in this direction, but had only gone a short distance when we realised (as all those others had before us) that the things we carried hampered us greatly. We would not abandon the basket containing Kitty, of course, and I was most reluctant to leave my green taffeta gown and my canvas bag, but we decided that the two boxes of kitchen things could be left, for they were easy enough to replace and had no great value. Seeing at this moment a woman running along the street screaming, her long hair alight from a falling brand, I made sure to tie my curls back and got Anne to cover them tight with a cloth for, although I did not like red hair, I would rather have it than be bald.

By leaving these kitchen stuffs inside another church we found it a little easier to get along. Still, though, there was the constant roar of the fire at our heels, a blizzard of sparks and firebrands falling over us, and shouted reports that 'There is no water left in the City!', 'Guildhall is a sea of flame!' and 'The water in the Fleet ditch is boiling!', each new cry serving to send us into more of a panic.

Nearing Moorgate and seeing the press of people converging on it from the surrounding streets, I began to despair of getting through.

'A carriage is in the gateway and stuck fast against a cart coming in!' a woman told us. 'We've been here near an hour without moving.'

I sighed mightily at this, for I felt responsible for Anne. 'I fear we've come to the wrong gate,' I said to her. 'I wish I had decided on Cripplegate.'

'There's a crowd fighting at Cripplegate,' said the woman. 'I heard two people have been stabbed over a tin of gold coins.'

'At Bishopsgate there are more people trying to get in and rescue goods than—' another began, but we never heard more, for of a sudden there was a huge roar and something must have given way at the gate, for the crowd in front of us surged forward and Anne's hand was wrenched from mine.

'Keep hold of Kitty's basket!' I shouted to her. 'Never mind about anything else. Make for Moore Fields, stay close to the walls and I'll find you!'

I believed that Anne got through for, as the great swell of people split, some surging one way, some the other, I glanced back and saw her being carried out of the gate by sheer force of numbers. I prayed that she would be safe, but did not know whether or not God still listened.

Now came my darkest time, for I was picked off my feet by the incoming mob and, after having all the breath squeezed out of me so I could neither scream nor hardly breathe, was shoved and manhandled, then knocked to the floor and somewhat trampled on. Several other people were used so, yet I did not feel that anyone meant this, rather that panic overtook the mass of people and the less robust among the crowd suffered the consequences.

Once the dense crowd had receded somewhat, I lay where I had been washed up, testing my limbs one by one and feeling where I had been hurt, and eventually I came to understand that I had no broken bones and was merely bruised and grazed. My green taffeta gown had disappeared, however, and also my canvas bag. A shawl that had been around my shoulders was also missing, and one shoe, but – my hand sprang to my neck and I gave a gasp of relief – my silver locket was still around my neck and my pocket containing our money was still under my petticoats.

As I struggled to lift my weary body from the cobbles, a young woman came along, her hair knotted and her face covered in smuts, and, sitting down beside me, began to cry.

'I've lost everything!' she said. 'My little house . . . my husband . . . all gone in fire so fierce it was as if the jaws of Hell had opened!'

I could not reply to her, for a stupor had come over me and I felt as tired as a dog.

'We thought we were safe, and then the fire dropped on us like a flaming sword from heaven! My husband stayed to fight it and I saw him consumed in the flames.'

'I . . . I'm sorry,' I said, struggling to get myself upright.

'His clothes, his hair, his face – all alight!' Her face came nearer to mine and she smiled sweetly. 'God chose him for an angel and then lit the cleansing fire around him!'

And now I struggled even harder to get on my feet, for I knew the woman to be mad and did not wish to get involved with her. My one thought was to get out of the City and find Anne. Getting to my feet unsteadily I left the woman crying at the side of the roadway and went on, luckily finding my shoe some distance away.

Discovering myself some little distance from Moorgate, I thought it best to try and make my way to a gate to the east of the City, which – as far as I knew – the fire had not yet reached. If I could go out of the City by Bishopsgate, then I could make my way into Moore Fields from there.

It was not that easy, however, for due to the heavy pall of smoke which hung over everything, I could hardly see in front of me and, not being able to recognise the lanes (for I was not often in this area) or see the sun, I could not work out the right direction to take. Some streets that I sought to go down had been closed off by the bands of men who had come together to earn the king's shilling, or they were impassable because of dumped goods or rubble. I turned my ankle and cut it on some sharp stones, was once made sick with coughing, and then was grazed badly by a runaway horse and cart which passed too close to me and then overturned. As well as this my eyes stung constantly and I often had to stop to shake out my skirts when a shower of sparks threatened to catch me alight.

Looking for landmarks, I found that many of these had disappeared and, thinking to find the tavern at the start of the great Lothbury highway which would lead me to Bishopsgate, found instead just a great heap of rubble where buildings had been pulled down with grappling irons. I asked directions, and if this was indeed Lothbury, but people were too frantic with their own matters to pay attention to me, and twice I was directed wrongly and came up against a wall of flame.

Feeling dizzy and by now desperate for water, I stopped a woman with a flask to beg a mouthful from it. She would not allow me any, however, and called me a careless hussy to come out without, saying she needed every drop for herself.

The day grew darker still and the wind began to rage like a beast, the smoke overhead growing thicker and more dense by every minute. Having no idea of where I was or what time it was, I began to be mighty scared, but stepping near to some ruined shops and crunching across lukewarm ashes, suddenly found myself near to St Paul's and felt a sense of relief. While much around this great church had already been laid to waste, and while other buildings still had flames licking up their stonework, St Paul's was built on a hill and looked to be invincible, standing aloft like a mighty castle.

Stumbling through its open doors I found that scores of people had also thought to find shelter there, and many had brought their animals and goods along, too, for I saw a pig, some dogs and a monkey along the wooden pews. Sinking on to a bench, weak with relief, I was given a cup of rough wine and a hard biscuit by a woman, both of which I would have scorned in normal times but now was very glad to accept. I slid into a quiet corner, closed my eyes and tried to quell my beating heart, for I had been traipsing the streets a very long while and felt as exhausted as a hunted deer.

In spite of the clamour within and without, I fell asleep for some minutes, and only awoke when the same woman shook me hard and told me that I must stir myself and flee.

'Surely not!' I said, my eyelids dropping once more. 'We are safe here.'

'If you do not stir you will be burned to death where you lie!' the woman chastised me. 'A flaming brand has fallen on this roof and even His house cannot protect you now.'

This, of course, roused me up and I ventured with a group of others towards a set of doors. Looking out I could see that a flaming circle surrounded us, for even those buildings which had seemed to be gutted now burned with a new lust. So many were the buildings which had been destroyed between my standpoint and the river that when the wind blew and the smoke and flames shifted a little I could see all the way through to the banks of Southwarke, which was very shocking and strange indeed.

Many of those who had been sheltering with me had already fled, taking their chance and looking for a break in the flames to run to safety, and I knew that I had to do the same if I wanted to survive.

Frightened, shivering in spite of the vindictive heat, I looked about me. The dark shroud of smoke above had grown more dense and oily as the fires raged all around, and was now churning like hot black oil. Suddenly, out of its depths, forked lightning began to stab all around, its following thunder almost lost in the terrible roar of the flames and howling wind. Instead of rain, however, the showers that fell were of golden sparks.

Whatever it was that had fallen on the roof of St Paul's must have suddenly flared, for a screaming came from a group of people some distance off and, with one accord, they turned to look back at the vast edifice which sheltered me, pointing at the roof and shouting in awe.

I knew I must run for my life, but the flames scorched all around and I was mighty scared, for such was the glare from these that I could not see what I was running to, and moreover was feared that a lightning fork might come down and strike me dead. I took three steps forward and two back, then started off in a different direction, only to run back again and again, too much affrighted to make a decision.

Four further steps forward . . . then again back, and I screamed aloud in frustration and despair, not knowing what to do for the best. Tears coursed down my cheeks, for I felt now that I was doomed to perish in this church and never to see Tom or my family again.

It was then, at my lowest moment, that I heard the voice that was to save me.

'Mistress!' someone shouted. 'Hannah!'

Dashing my tears aside, I saw by the light of the encroaching flames the silhouette of a lad standing with a small, laden handcart before him. 'Who is that?' I called.

''Tis I, Hannah. Bill!'

But this meant nothing to me and I still could not see him, for the flames were as bright as sun in my eyes.

'Bill! Don't you remember me? Lord Cartmel's bootboy!' the figure shouted. 'Jump on my cart, Mistress!'

My befuddled brain could still not understand who it was who addressed me, and I wavered and swayed and would have fallen on to the smouldering grass, but the lad dropped the handles of the cart and ran to me. Catching me under the arms, he dragged me towards the cart, then kicked a deal of books from it and dropped me on to it without further ceremony.

With me clinging on as best I could, he then began trundling me over the stones and rubble away from St Paul's, faster and faster, until I cried aloud for him to stop to enable me to catch my breath. Even this did not halt him, however, and he did not pause until we had reached a safe place away from the flames.

Here he breathlessly pointed towards St Paul's, shaking his head the while, and sitting up on the cart I could see flames rising at the edge of the great roof, and from this point catching all over and darting in every direction, different colours according to the material they burned: red, orange, yellow, white and gold, each stretching up to the dense fire-storm cloud above. Within just a few moments large parts of the roof, stone and burning timber, fell inwards and the whole cathedral became a roaring cauldron of fire.

Speechlessly we watched as this maelstrom of fury began to melt the lead roof of the cathedral, which then began to flow in silvery streams, sparkling and flashing, making everything it touched erupt in darting pinnacles of flame. Suddenly, like pistol shots, the great windows began to shatter and flames burst through. At this point the heat and brightness of the great fire became so intense that, although we were a good distance off, we had to move or our skin would have blistered.

Both exhausted, we stopped at last in a thoroughfare where the heat from the fire could not touch us, and I knew that my saviour was indeed Bill, Lord Cartmel's bootboy. Realising this, I somehow mustered the strength to fling my arms around him and sob out my thanks for saving me, for I knew that I would not have had the courage to run through that ring of flames and save myself.

'But what are you *doing* here?' I asked when I had left off my speeches of gratitude.

'Making a pretty penny!' he said. 'I'm a beast of burden with a cart for hire and I've been charging the gentry two pounds a load to take their furniture and treasures away to safety out of the City.' His smutty face grinned at me. 'I've made myself a fair fortune in the last two days!'

'But where is your master?'

'Oh, he high-tailed it to Dorchester at the first sign of danger, leaving me and two footmen to clear his house.' He rubbed his hands. 'I tell you, Mistress, I'm a made man! I've earned enough money in this last two days to marry and live in luxury for the rest of my life!'

He winked at me and I knew where his thoughts were heading and sought to distract him. 'Bill,' I pleaded, 'could I ask you for one more thing – to help me find my sister? I told her I'd meet her by the wall in Moore Fields but don't know how to get there.'

'Oh, that's easy!' he boasted. 'The route out of the City is drawn in my head, for I've now done it fifty times or more. But we'll not go through Moorgate but by way of Aldgate in the east.'

And so we set off across the City at a steadier pace – with me riding on the cart like a pig going to market, for he would not let me walk – and only stopped once more: when there was, of a sudden, a tremendous noise from the west and a moment later the whole of the City was lit up with a glow as bright as the noonday sun.

''Tis the crypt below St Paul's,' Bill said grimly. 'The booksellers have packed it full of their precious papers and books and now the fire has reached down there and 'tis all exploded into flame.'

After surveying the roaring and flickering city scene before us – the great heaps of rubble, the piles of ash, the charred stone and, nearby, some vast oak church beams glowing red like coals – we commenced our journey to Moore Fields, for I think Bill was anxious to install me in a place of safety so that he could carry on making his fortune.

Chapter Twelve

Moore Fields

'Going to the fire, I find, by the blowing up of houses and the great help given by the workmen out of the King's yards, there is a good stop given to it . . .'

When I opened my eyes in Moore Fields the following morning, it was to find Anne sitting close at my side looking down at me anxiously.

'You've been asleep for hours!' she said. 'You were curled up like a cat and I didn't like to wake you.'

I looked up at her blankly, as for some moments I could not recall where I was or how I came to be there.

'And if you *are* a cat, then you're a very dirty one!' Anne went on. 'Your gown is filthy, your hair is singed and matted. You look like a sweep and stink worse than a glue-maker!'

I sat bolt-upright and looked around, suddenly remembering where I was – in that hummocky, shrubby place where the laundresses of the City took their sheets and hung them on the bushes to dry. There were no sheets there now, however, for their place had been taken by hundreds – nay, thousands – of people sitting, lying or standing, together with their furniture, bundles, baskets, books and animals, and all so cramped that there was scarcely a space between them.

'However did you find me?' I asked Anne in astonishment.

She smiled. ''T'was easy!' she said. 'I fell in with the McGibbons family last night, and at first light this morning I told their six children what you were wearing – although I did not know your gown would have changed *quite* so much – and said that I would give a paper cone of sweetmeats to the one who found you.'

I looked around for the McGibbons, who owned a small pie shop a few doors away from us in Crown and King Place, but for the moment could not see them amid the crush.

'The children took off at first light and by searching diligently along the walls, found you within a half hour!' Anne shook her head ruefully. 'I don't know when I'll be able to pay them the sweetmeats, though . . .'

I gasped. 'Has the fire then reached our shop?'

She nodded solemnly. 'Mistress McGibbon told me that it reached Crown and King Place late last afternoon. There was a trained band of men there and they pulled down the houses behind ours with grappling irons to try and save our row, but the flames leaped across the gap and . . .' She stopped, seeing my eyes brim with tears, and after a moment went on, 'No lives lost, though, Hannah. And look!' She lifted a corner of her skirt and there was Kitty, fast asleep on the grass with a ribbon around her neck, the end of which was tied around Anne's wrist.

I smiled, but it was only a very small smile. We had lost everything – everything except Kitty and the clothes we stood up in – and even *those* were ruined and torn. My hand once again flew to my neck and my smile lightened a little, for I still wore my precious locket – moreover, I knew my pocket was still tied under my skirts, for I could feel the little swell of money resting on my hip.

'But our little shop, though!' I said, picturing its pretty sign, its wooden shutters and limewashed interior. 'Our shop all gone to ashes . . . What will Sarah say? She left me in charge of it.'

'Hannah!' Anne exclaimed. 'She won't say a thing. She'll just be happy that both of us are safe. And how could you have preserved *our* little shop when the greatest buildings in the city have caught fire?'

I sighed and nodded. 'I saw St Paul's alight,' I said. 'What a sight it was, Anne – a great box of fire lighting up the sky and turning it into day. 'T'was hot enough nearby to cook a thousand turkeys.'

'They say that all the big buildings have gone, and thousands of smaller houses besides. The prisons, too – and poor mad people left to burn in their chains!'

I turned away with a shudder. 'Don't!'

'But tell me how you came to be here,' Anne said, 'for I stayed close to the wall as you told me, and watched and watched people coming through the gate until it was grew dark – although it didn't really grow dark because of all the flames – but I never saw you come in.'

'I'll tell you soon, but I have not the heart to talk yet,' I said. 'And I'm fair famished! Is there anything to eat anywhere?'

'There's some ship's biscuit,' Anne said, 'though it's nasty and salty and hard. But there are folk coming in from the country today with fruit and beer and milk to sell, and the king has promised that no one will go hungry.'

'Really? How could he promise that?' I asked, looking across the field where, as far as the eye could see, people were crowded into makeshift camps. 'There must be people holed up in every single safe place outside the City. How will he feed them all?'

Anne shrugged. 'I don't know. *He's* the king, not me.'

We sat there for a very long time, for I felt weary and befuddled – and besides, there was nowhere to go. Occasionally news would come to us of what was now burning, what had been burned down or of where the fire had been stopped. Smoke blew across the walls, eddied around and hung over us, and smuts and burning brands swirled and dropped all around. On the other side of the walls we could hear the fire roaring and the wind blowing, and booming and cracking from different directions where they were blowing up houses with gunpowder, followed by the tumbling crash of falling stone.

By the afternoon of that day, however, which was Wednesday, the news came to us that the wind was blowing itself out. Later still, we heard that the fires in most directions had been extinguished, while those that still burned were thought to be under control.

This information ran around the whole of Moore Fields until it reached every far corner, but there was very little delight or joy shown, for we were all dreadful tired, hungry and disorientated and, as most had already lost their homes and possessions, it meant little. We took in the news and were pleased about it, but could display no emotion. The only time any feeling was shown was when some citizen or other, hearing a rumour, would try and rouse others, calling, 'To arms! To arms!' and giving out that a Frenchman had started the fire, or a Dutchman, or any foreigner at all. During the day we heard many such tales, and also that a man seen throwing fire balls into a shop had been torn limb from limb by the crowd, and that a woman who had predicted the fire had been killed for a witch, but I did not know whether these things were true.

'What will we do?' Anne asked me frequently during the day. 'What will become of us?'

Each time she asked I shook my head, for I just did not know. I felt, too, that I was not qualified, nor hardly old enough, to have to deal with such questions, and wished desperately that Sarah were with us so that I would not have to be the one to make any decisions.

Anne looked dishevelled but was not too far off from her normal self; though she kept looking at me and smiling with some amusement at *my* appearance. Seeing this, I asked leave to borrow a looking-glass from a family we were alongside, and had the shock of seeing what I had become.

'I'm a scabby, sooty, dirty beggar!' I said, holding the glass this way and that and looking at my reflection in shock.

'Indeed you are,' Anne said. 'I don't think even your

sweetheart would recognise you.'

'Have you anything – a cloth or a kerchief I could wipe myself with?' I asked.

She shook her head. 'Nor a comb to de-tangle your hair, or soap to clean you or any flower water to hide the smell of soot on you.' As I uttered a sigh of protest, she added, 'But everyone looks the same, Hannah. You won't be noticed.'

The mention of Tom had spurred me into action and at length, not finding any other cloth, I tore a strip from my undersmock and, walking around the perimeter of the field, wetted this material in a stream. On instruction from Anne on where the worst dirt was, I then began to clean myself as best I could. The singed eyebrows I could do nothing about, nor the bruise on my cheek, nor my hair which, to my despair, had tangled into a vast red cloud, but I managed to get all the smuts from my face and felt the better for it – even if I did not actually look much better.

By and by, people were seen coming round with trays of food from the naval storehouse, and everyone fell to cheering, but these trays proved only to contain more of the hard ship's biscuit which no one liked. Anne and I took some, however, and after eating a little ourselves, pounded up the rest for Kitty and she was glad enough to have it. Others in the Fields fed their dogs with it, and the McGibbons family – who had thought to bring along three chickens from their backyard – fed the biscuit to them and hoped thus to ensure a couple of fresh eggs each day for their children.

We heard later that day that the king had ordered the magistrates and lieutenants of the surrounding counties to ensure that all the food that could be spared, especially bread, should be sent immediately to London, and that temporary markets were to be set up for this just beyond the burned areas at Smithfield, Bishopsgate and Tower Hill. As well as this, any City bakers who had not been gutted by fire were ordered to bake bread around the clock, and extra grain was to be made available for this purpose. These loaves were later brought into Moore Fields, and we managed to obtain some small beer and also milk, and in this way kept ourselves going. I thought often of the sweetmeats and comfits that we had left behind in the shop, and wished that I had thought to put some of them in my pocket. Other shopkeepers, though, had left behind far more costly things: bales of silken fabrics bought ready for the Michaelmas fairs, rare books, boxes of scented gloves from Persia, gold coins (which we heard had melted and fused together in the heat) or silver plates destined for the same fate – so we counted ourselves lucky to have left behind only frosted rose petals and sugared plums.

By that evening we were assured that, although fires still burned in some cellars and warehouses, these would not now spread further. We were urged to stay on the Fields, however, until it was quite safe to move. This suited me very well, for I felt mighty fatigued still and could not have dealt with moving. I just wanted to sit where I was on the grass and feel safe, and not think about what was going to happen next.

As night came, it was the strangest thing to go to sleep (or try to sleep) amongst such a vast company and in such strange circumstances. As far as the eye could see, people were now packed head to tail across the grass, sitting or lying down, squeezed into corners with whatever stuff they had managed to bring with them: a bundle of clothes, say, or a chair or wash stand, a cloth containing food, the household pig or some small treasure. A few had also managed to bring a candle or taper along, so that, as darkness fell across the field, a number of flickering lights appeared, and these reflected off people's faces and lit up the field into a huge and peculiar landscape the like of which can hardly be imagined.

Although desperately weary, we could hardly close our eyes because of the very strangeness of it all: the sounds of shouting, wailing, children crying, dogs barking – and every so often from the other side of the wall, the far-off rumble of a damaged house falling, mingled with screams, or the shooting of sparks into the sky where a thatch had suddenly caught fire.

As it grew darker it grew colder, so that although Anne and I curled up as close as a pair of spoons, we became chilled as the damp rose from the earth. There were other dangers apart from cold, too, for the enormity of what had happened to the City had not changed the essential part of some people's wicked characters, and loose fellows prowled around looking for unguarded objects to steal; indeed I fell asleep once, only to wake at feeling a fellow's hand under my skirts and upon my pocket. I sat up immediately and shouted abuse and he ran off into the darkness.

Thus, managing to sleep only now and again, we passed the night, not knowing what would become of us.

The following morning there was some excitement and lightening of mood when the king himself came to speak to us. A fanfare of trumpets sounded his arrival, then the crowds parted and he, attended by a few gentlemen, wearing an elegant riding jacket and sitting atop his fine black horse, spoke about the dilemma that the City found itself in.

'The judgement which has fallen upon London is immediately from the hand of God, for be assured that no Frenchmen, Dutchmen or Catholics had any part in bringing you so much misery,' he said in a clear and decisive tone. 'I assure you that I find no reason to suspect anyone's involvement in burning the City, and desire you to take no more alarm. I, your king, will, by the Grace of God, live and die with you, and take a particular care of you all.'

We were all much moved by this and, as he went off to speak to another group, many of us shed tears at his kind words and chivalrous intentions (and I am sure did not give one thought to his indiscretions or bastard children). Anne was particularly overcome by him and spoke admiringly of his princely manner, looks and virility, saying she thought him the most noble man alive.

That afternoon we heard that, to prevent the remaining small fires gaining more of a foothold, a detachment of two hundred soldiers was coming from Hertfordshire with carts laden with spades and buckets. Everyone at Moore Fields was very glad to hear this, for we were all exhausted and a great lassitude had crept over us. I dreamed of nothing more than being back in my bed-chamber in Chertsey, in clean clothes, with Mother bathing my grazes and making me soothing camomile drinks. This lovely vision, however, seemed as far off and impossible as the one promised by Count de'Ath on entering his cabinet.

Chapter Thirteen

The Devastated City

'By water to St Paul's wharf. Walked thence and saw all the town burned, and a miserable sight of Paul's church, with all the roofs fallen and the body of the quire fallen . . .'

On Friday and Saturday the move back into the City began, for the lethargy that had fallen on everyone had somewhat passed, and by then most of us were anxious to see what remained of London now that the fire was halted, and whether or not anything survived of our homes. Those re-entering the City were asked to be vigilant, to watch for anything suspicious and to stamp out any glowing embers they might see so that they wouldn't catch flame.

Faced with having to move on, some now chose not to go back into the City at all, saying they could not bear seeing the calamity which had befallen their homes and possessions. These folk started journeying on foot to wherever they could, to places where they had family or friends and could mayhap start again, for it had been decreed that cities and towns everywhere must receive and welcome distressed refugees from London and permit them to trade.

I could not decide what to do. Although I longed for home, I didn't want to leave London without getting word to Tom and telling him where I'd gone. Also, knowing there was little chance of obtaining a lift on a carriage or a cart, we could not yet face making the arduous trek to Chertsey on foot. We were very weary, for we'd slept little on the Fields because of the continuous noise and movement from those around us, and also the alarms sounding whenever wind-blown firebrands came over the walls. Besides, when I'd slept, I'd had terrible nightmares that I was once again in the doorway of St Paul's with the ring of flames all around me and about to burn to death. Each time, I woke to Anne shaking me and telling me I was crying out in my sleep, and was glad she did so, for I had this childish superstition that if I actually fell asleep and dreamed I was dead, then I would not ever wake.

Eventually (Anne being very anxious to do so) I decided we would go back to Crown and King Place and see if anything remained of our shop. Once we had seen it, we could then decide if we should stay put and start again – for we'd heard that several people had already put up rough stands or tents upon the rubble and ashes of their former homes, and some few were already trading by obtaining provisions from outside London to sell.

Accordingly, with Kitty safely inside her basket, we set off, going through Moorgate, where two burly guards had been posted to stop thieves coming out with stolen goods. We knew that there was much looting and pillaging taking place in the City, for treasures that had been sealed up in cellars, buried in gardens or left in the few houses which had survived the fire were now ripe for the taking. Guards were also on duty about the City ready to quell any disturbances between the citizens and foreigners for, in spite of what the king had said, people were still not certain of how the fire had started, but were mighty anxious to place the blame somewhere.

We'd already glimpsed the devastation through Moorgate, but this did not prepare us for the spectacle we saw when we were past the walls and into the open space beyond them.

For this is what it was: an open space. As far as the eye could see, from the City walls right down to the Thames, all was laid to waste, with little to be seen but random heaps of rubble and stones under a sifting, shifting layer of ash. There were no grassy squares or winding cobbled lanes or dim passageways . . . the beautiful city with its pretty houses, grand buildings and ancient churches stood no more.

Anne and I surveyed it all, and I felt too heavy to speak, for I had never seen such desolation and could hardly comprehend how it was possible for such a thing to have happened and for such a mighty city to have fallen.

'Where do we go from here?' Anne spoke at last, but I just shook my head wordlessly, for all landmarks had gone and without those it seemed impossible to trace where our shop had been.

We walked on a little further, to where the remains of a church stood. This, being of heavy stone, had somewhat survived, for although the roof and windows had disappeared (there just being some traces of red- and blue-stained glass melted and fused into the ground nearby), remains of the spire still stood, and at least a part of each wall.

'What church is this?' Anne asked.

I stood looking at it doubtfully. 'St Alphage, I think,' I said. 'Although I don't know this parish well.'

We walked on. 'And if so . . .' I pointed to two great heaps of smoking rubble, 'here was Clothworkers' Hall . . . and over there, Brewers' Hall.'

We stood silent once more, lost in thought. Around us from several places rose thin spires of smoke. Further off, a grey and steamy fogginess seemed to hang over all, and through this could be seen dismal figures such as ourselves, picking their way over the ashes like so many grey ghosts. As soft ash floated up with each movement, making us cough, piles of dirt and dust eddied about any remaining stumps of walls. There was black soot-dirt from burned wood, grey dirt from the reduced stones and red and yellow dirt from the bricks that had caught aflame. In places where it had been blown by circles of wind this detritus was inches thick, and looking at it I could not think how it would ever be possible to make London clean again.

Anne came and put her hand through mine. 'I don't like it,' she said tremulously. 'Shall we go home to Mother?'

I squeezed her hand. 'If we can,' I said. 'But let's try and find Crown and King Place. Just in case . . .'

Just in case . . . I knew not what. Just in case there had been a lull in the fire and it had jumped right over our row of shops and left them intact. Just in case a trained band had obtained fire squirts and directed them on to our shop so that it had escaped. Miracles *did* sometimes happen, I already knew that.

Working from St Alphage, we made our way through the wreckage towards where we thought our shop had been. On the way we saw some small signs of revival: a man who had made a table from two planks of wood and was selling beer from it, and another who had fashioned a rough tent from some canvas and had set up home on what remained of his dwelling. One family also seemed to be living in the cellar of what had been their house, for the trap door to this was open, voices came from below, and a child was seated atop, playing forlornly amid a pile of cinders.

A man stopped us to say that owing to an order of the king, all churches, chapels and other public places in the east of the City that had survived were open freely to receive goods that might be brought to them for safekeeping.

I thanked him as he passed on. 'But we have nothing to leave in them,' I said to Anne.

'Just Kitty,' she said.

People had reached what had been their houses and were standing inside, looking lost and bewildered. I saw very few tears, however, for people seemed too shocked for that. Some, finding their own places, had pinned a paper to a blackened stave of wood, or left word on a pile of stones to say what shop it was, or had hung a piece of material or some object (I saw a quill, and later a pewter mug) to denote what had once stood there.

We moved on and, by careful register of what

remained of churches and some Halls of the Guilds, found our way through the remains of the City to what was left of Crown and King Place. Here we surveyed where our little row of shops and houses had stood, and I knew then that a miracle had *not* happened, and that our shop had been laid to waste and destroyed utterly, along with all the others, and I felt very sad and low.

Here, too, we found Mr Newbery sitting on a stump of wood inside what had been his premises, a tankard in his hand. He had no wig, nor even proper dress, but was wearing an old, loose Indian robe such as those worn by gentlemen of leisure at home. This gown was torn and dishevelled, however, and was spotted all over with small burn marks, as if he had walked through a shower of sparks whilst wearing it.

He rose and gave us a slight bow, swaying on his feet. 'Ah! You found your way back, then,' he said, with as much ease as if he had been receiving us in his parlour. I nodded, staring at him (as I knew Anne was), for his bald pate had big smuts of soot all over it and his cheeks seemed to be liberally powdered with grey ash. 'It took me a good long time to get myself here, for all the taverns are down and I couldn't work out where I was.'

'Did our neighbours all survive? Have you seen anyone?' I asked him.

'Oh, several,' he said. 'Few have died.' He then added in his usual manner, 'Although I heard that at Bridewell the flames raged with such intolerable heat that the very dead in their graves were burnt!' and I could not help smiling to myself at this.

'Are you going to stay here?' Anne asked him.

He nodded. 'I managed to preserve my clothes and some of my goods by taking them to a friend in Bishopsgate. He boxed them and buried them in his garden for safekeeping, and luckily the fire did not get that far.'

'But where will you live?' I asked.

'Soldiers are erecting makeshift tents for people, so I shall retrieve my goods and begin trading again as soon as I can. I want to be here to give directions for the rebuilding of my shop.'

'I see,' I said, and then asked to be excused, adding that we were mighty anxious to go inside our own place.

'Oh, not a thing remains of it!' he called after us.

Our shop had been separated from his by two small and mean dwellings. These were now no more, and a half-stump of oak was all that was left of our doorjamb. This was charcoaled and reduced, but meant we could see where our premises began. Shuffling around the debris on the ground with our feet (which we had to do with care, some of the ashes still being hot), the outline of the floor could be seen, and the division into the back room; also, oddly, a burnt stub of the sturdy bush of rosemary which had stood in our yard.

I cannot explain how strange it felt to be standing in our shop – and yet not our shop, for it was filled with debris from the roof and upper floor, and open to the skies. To the right we could look along to where Mr Newbery could be seen drinking from his tankard, and to the left could be glimpsed, through the devastated houses, the broken spire and ruins of our parish church.

Kitty, who usually remained quiet whenever she was in her basket, suddenly started to meow, as if knowing she was home, but of course we did not dare let her out.

'There's a note here, pinned to a strut of wood!' Anne said suddenly.

'Really?' I moved to her quickly, my long skirts making the dust lift and swirl. 'Let me see.'

This small piece of parchment was nailed to a charred brace, and I removed it carefully, my heart pounding, for I could already see that it was in Sarah's careful script.

I read it out:

'Having heard of the dreadful fire, we are come to London and I wait with Giles Copperly to bring you and Anne back to Chertsey. As we may not bring the carriage into the City, the ways all being blocked with rubble, we stay on the Southwarke side and will remain here until you come to us. Please God that you are both safe. Your sister Sarah.'

Thinking of my elder sister waiting on the other side of the river for us, anxious for news, made my eyes brim with tears, and I turned away to dab at them with a piece of my skirt.

Anne uttered a long sigh and then pulled at my sleeve. 'Oh, can we go now?' she implored me, and a moment later added, 'A carriage belonging to Giles Copperly! Do you think he and Sarah are betrothed?'

I shook my head unknowingly.

'There's no reason at all to stay here now!' Anne went on. ''Tis awful and I hate it and we can't possibly make sweetmeats *here*!'

'I know,' I said, biting my lip. I was anxious to get away too, but reluctant to go without telling Tom. Looking down at Sarah's note, however, I thought immediately of what I could do – employ the same method as she had and leave a few lines in case he should come by.

I had no quill, of course, and sought to borrow one from Mr Newbery, but he told me that all his presently lay buried in the strongbox in his friend's garden.

'I shall pin Sarah's own note back to the wall, then,' I said to him, 'so it should be clear enough that we've gone to Chertsey. If anyone comes for me then please direct them to it.'

'Indeed I shall!' Mr Newbery said rather grandly, and with a slur to his voice, making me wonder how much ale he had already drunk that day.

'We hope to see you again soon, Mr Newbery,' I said. 'Although I don't know when.'

He waved the tankard. 'Be assured that if any other young man asks after you, I shall tell him where you've gone.'

I'd already turned away when what he'd said registered with my fuddled brain: if any *other* young man . . . 'Has someone asked for me already, then?'

'A lad came a while back. In quite a mess, he was!' He glugged his ale. 'Been in a fight, I should imagine.'

'What did he want?' My heart was fluttering but I fought to stay calm. Had it been Tom – or only Bill? Had I told him where the shop was that night at St Paul's?

Mr Newbery shrugged. 'He just asked for you and I

told him I hadn't seen you, neither dead nor alive.'

'And where did he go? In which direction?' I asked urgently.

Mr Newbery waved his tankard and ale slopped from it. 'Who knows. In the direction of wreckage and rubble.' He smiled, pleased with himself. 'For in every direction is wreckage and rubble!'

I left him then and, calling to Anne that I would be just a moment, hurried up the lane (as best I could because of the devastating ruins) towards the corner where Doctor da Silva's shop had stood. If it had indeed been Tom who'd asked for me I thought that, finding himself with nowhere else to go, he might make for the apothecary's shop where he'd once lived.

This was not too difficult to find, for it had stood at the convergence of several lanes, and the outlines of these could still be traced. Reaching what I thought was the remains of it, I had further confirmation that I was in the right place by seeing what was left of several heavy iron chains and padlocks from when the shop had been enclosed in the plague time. This ironwork was in a heap on the ground, fused together by the heat which had passed over it.

Scrambling over stones I found Tom lying within the rubble, propped against some brickwork. His knees were drawn up, his head down on them, and he gave no indication of having heard my arrival.

I gasped with shock at the sight of him for, as well as being covered in dirt and ash, through his torn and bloodied shirt I could see dark bruises across his shoulders and large abrasions on his back.

'Tom!' I called.

He lifted his head and gave me a weak smile, then

closed his eyes. 'Excuse me not rising, Hannah.'

'What happened to you?' I put out my hand to touch his shoulder, causing him to wince. 'Did you fall from a carriage or – or get in a fight?'

He shook his head and sighed wearily. 'It isn't a pretty tale.' There was a pause. 'I was stoned by a mob.' I gasped. 'Along with Count de'Ath – although I should not call him that because that isn't his real name – and it was that which led to the trouble.'

I looked at him and longed to put my arms around him, for he looked so broken, but I was scared of hurting him. '*Stoned?*'

He nodded and explained in a croak. 'We – some of the folk of Bartholomew Fair – had moved on to the common land in Islington. Local men got to hear that Count de'Ath was there, and, thinking him a Frenchman, sought him out and were about to take him and hang him, saying it was he and his compatriots who had caused the fire.'

He paused to take several slow breaths, then went on, 'A soldier intervened and stopped them, saying it could not be proved that anyone started it, and for his pains was stoned out of the village with us.' He paused again here and I stroked his face tenderly, for there was a small space on his cheek which wasn't bruised.

'The Count jumped on a horse and galloped off, and most of the mob ran after him, leaving me to evade the rest and walk back here. I didn't know where else to go.'

'You must come back with us!' I said immediately. 'Sarah is waiting at Southwarke with a carriage, and we are going home to Chertsey.'

'I cannot . . .' he protested weakly.

"You must!' I said. 'Tom, I insist.' My mind raced ahead. 'You will be able to obtain lodgings in our village. And work, too, later, if you wish.'

He did not say anything, but he looked at me with such great relief that my eyes filled with tears again for pity of him.

'Come now,' I said, and I put my hand under his arm to help him to his feet. 'We shall have a grand ride home in a carriage and—'

He let out a cry and clutched his elbow. 'I fear I shall not be good for work with a broken arm.'

'You will mend!' I said with false cheer, but seeing him standing, I hid my dismay at the pitiful, wretched sight he made. His arm hung useless, fine ash had stuck to his open wounds, and his skin, where visible, was blue with bruising. 'You shall have the root and leaves of comfrey to mend your broken bone, and alkanet and pennyroyal to heal the bruises and cuts. You know the herbs as well as I do!'

He tried to smile at me and just about succeeded. Slowly then, with his good arm about my shoulders, we made our way down towards Crown and King Place. We passed other citizens who were either shocked, burnt, dirty, troubled, dazed – or all of those things – but none spoke, nor hardly looked at us with any interest, for everyone was deep in their own troubles and woes, and much brought down with them.

At Crown and King Place Mr Newbery was not now to be seen, but Anne was standing by, looking anxious. On seeing Tom's condition, her eyes widened and she gasped. 'Did you get caught in the fire?' she asked. 'What happened?'

'We'll tell you on the journey,' I said. 'We're taking Tom back home with us. He has nowhere to go. And no work,' I added.

'Perhaps he can work with Father,' she said. 'He's always complaining he has too much to do.'

'Perhaps,' I nodded.

Anne went to take Tom's other, broken, arm but I shook my head at her. 'You manage Kitty, I'll manage Tom.'

Leaving what remained of our shop then, we began to walk very slowly, passing others trudging at a snail's pace and looking around them in bewildered fashion. In the ash-fogged light we were all grey wraiths, moving through a wasteland of rubble and stones. Twice we came across still-glowing coals and directed passing soldiers to stamp them out, and going by what remained of St Dominic's we found that the tower was down, its great lead bells melted completely and fused into the stones in a strange, mountainous lump.

Once or twice on our journey Tom swayed and almost fainted and we had to sit on the ground for a while until he recovered, but pretty soon we came in sight of London Bridge and I knew there would soon be an end to his ordeal.

It was while we were waiting our turn to get on to the bridge through the narrow passage that had been forged between the heaps of wreckage, that Anne slid her hand into Kitty's basket and drew something out. 'While I was waiting for you, I looked around in our shop and found this,' she said.

I took what she offered and gasped with surprise,

for I saw that it was part of the metal sign which had hung above our shop. It was much reduced and had melted and buckled through the great heat, but a part of the painted image could still be seen. Gazing at it, I was torn between smiling and weeping. 'The sugared plum,' I whispered. 'To think that this is all that remains of our shop.'

Anne shrugged, murmuring that she'd thought I'd like to keep it, and Tom looked at me with sympathy. 'London will be rebuilt, and your shop along with it,' he reassured me gently. 'And when it is, I'll make you another sign.'

I smiled at him – indeed I would have kissed him had I been able to find space on his poor face – for I knew what he said about London was true. I felt that my fate was with Tom, but it was also with London, and one day we would return and there would be another shop, trading anew under the sign of the Sugared Plum.

But for now we would cross London Bridge, find Sarah and go home . . .

Notes on the Great Fire of London

The Great Fire of London began on Sunday 2nd September 1666 in Pudding Lane and was finally halted (some say at Pie Corner) by nightfall on Wednesday 5th September.

Year of the Beast In the Bible, 666 is the number of the beast, who has the ability to bring down fire from heaven. 1666 had long been heralded by hellfire preachers and puritans as the year when God's punishment would fall on sinful London.

Samuel Pepys All the quotations at the chapter headings, and some of the stories of the characters, are from Pepys's *Diary*. Pepys was perhaps the most famous observer of the fire and wrote movingly of it (he was also the man who buried a whole Parmesan cheese in his garden). Two other books I used were *The Great Fire of London* by W. G. Bell, first published in 1923, for its accurate detail, and *Restoration London* by Liza Picard, an amusing and invaluable source of background material.

Nell Gwyn was sixteen in 1666 and had been acting with the King's Company for a year. By 1668 she had become the king's mistress and two years after this she had a child by him. Strikingly attractive and a practical joker, Nelly never hid her humble beginnings and the people loved her for this.

Bartholomew Fair All the sideshows and stalls mentioned (and more) were at the real fair, which was held for two weeks at the end of August. I have taken liberties with history only in that Bartholomew Fair was not held in 1666, for fear there would be a reoccurrence of plague.

Numbers of deaths Early counts had it that only a handful of people perished in the fire, but now it is believed that many more may have died, for such was the disruption to ordinary life that there were no Bills of Mortality published for three weeks after the fire and so no way of telling just how many perished in that fierce, all-consuming heat.

Numbers of houses burnt It is thought that about 15,000 houses and Guild Halls were burnt, including some of the most palatial and beautiful buildings in the city, and about eighty churches, including St Paul's, of course. There was no such thing as fire insurance and no way of obtaining recompense for what had been lost.

Rebuilding It took many years to get back to some normality (St Paul's Cathedral was not completed until 1711) and for some years the rubble was occupied by shacks and alehouses built to entertain all the workmen employed on the rebuilding of London. Jetties (the fronts that jutted out from houses) were now banned, as were all-wood structures. The streets were also made wider to help prevent fires catching from one side to the other.

Plague One of the most commonly-held beliefs was that the fire 'finished off' the plague of the previous year. The truth is that plague had more or less ceased in London by September 1666, but what the fire did was to burn out the worst of the filthy, unsanitary and horrendously overcrowded buildings in which people lived (sometimes ten to a room), thus ensuring plague would find it difficult ever to get a foothold again.

Who started the fire? In October 1666 a Frenchman named Robert Hubert, who had confessed to starting the fire, was hung, but there were doubts at the time as to whether he was sane, or had even been in the country at the time. Many thought that Thomas Farriner, the baker in Pudding Lane, was responsible, because he had not guarded his fire well enough. Others thought Dutch, Spanish – or a group of Catholics – were to blame. The people of London were desperate enough to blame anyone, and religious and racial intolerance are not new.

Recipes from the Still Room

Most grand houses had a still room (the word 'still' comes from 'distilling'). Here the women of the household would prepare pot pourri, balms and scented waters, and distil flowers in order to obtain precious drops of their essential oils.

Rose water

Pot pourri

Herbal hair rinses

Scented water to bathe in

Pomander balls

Rose water

Gather petals from three or four full roses that have not been treated with pesticides. Place in a saucepan with a pint of water. Heat gently until the petals become transparent, but do not allow them to boil. Let the mixture cool, then strain through a sieve into a jug, pushing the petals with your fingers to extract all the liquid. Keep mixture in the fridge (it will keep for a week or so) and use as a cooling spray on face or body.

Pot pourri

Pick apart several full roses and dry out on a paper towel in a warm spot, turning them occasionally. Add dried marjoram, thyme, rosemary and lavender flowers or any other strongly scented herbs, plus the dried, chopped rind of an orange and a lemon. Add some dried bay leaves, cloves and a teaspoon of cinnamon. Mix well together and stir occasionally.

Herbal hair rinses

Using a herbal infusion to rinse your hair after washing will condition your hair and leave it shiny and sweet-smelling. Use a tablespoonful of dried herbs to two pints of boiling water, leave covered until cool, then strain and bottle. After washing and rinsing your hair, use a cupful or two of the infusion in a jug, pouring through your hair several times.

Thyme

Herbs to use

Camomile and dried marigold flowers will add highlights to light hair; sage works well on darker hair. Adding nettles and dried elderflowers will help combat dandruff. Lad's love (sometimes called southernwood), still to be found in cottage gardens and from herbalists, was a seventeenth-century remedy to make hair grow thicker and faster.

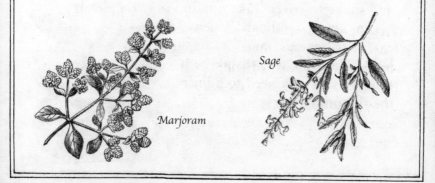

Marjoram

Sage

Scented water to bathe in

To one pint of water add eight tablespoons of dried herbs, or double this of fresh ones, mixing them according to whatever you have in abundance. Put into a pan and simmer gently for ten minutes, then cool completely and strain, pressing down the herbs to extract as much liquid as possible. Use a quarter of this mixture to scent your bath, and for an extra-special touch, scatter fresh petals on the water. As a guide, rose and lovage are cleansing and deodorising; rosemary and hyssop are refreshing; lime flowers and lavender are relaxing; and camomile and lemon balm are soothing.

Rosemary

Pomander balls

Can be made with any citrus fruit. Divide into sections and pin ribbon or lace around to mark the quarter-sections. Stud all over in straight lines with cloves (using a knitting needle first to make the holes), then place the fruit in a paper bag containing cinnamon and shake to cover. Take out and dry completely in an airing cupboard, then add extra trimmings and a hanging loop. The fruit will shrink as it dries so you may need to adjust the ribbon-markers.

Orange